AN EMOTIONAL HOMICIDE

FIRST EDITON

Perfect Pair
Publications,LLC.

BOOK TITLES
FROM
PERFECT PAIR PUBLICATIONS, ™

By. Bashan "BedStuy" Murchison (5.5x 5.8, paperback)

The "4" W's;

Who, What, When, Where;

Entertainment Directory.

The Truth;

A Real Prisoner Resource Guide.

Legal Conflict.

Lyrically Speaking.

Perfect Pair Singles.

The Tennessee Incarcerated Bad Girls.

P.O.W.

Prisoners of Words.

Always Loved Never Forgotten.

Ms. Voluptuous

and

By. Lorenzo Andrews (5.5 x 5.8, paperback)

An Emotional Homicide; Black Raspberry.

By. Eugene Beaird (5.5 x 5.8, paperback) **All Hustle No Love; 1,2, &,3**

Find us on the following social networks

WWW. Face book. Com/ Perfect Pair Publications

WWW. Twitter.com/ Perfect Pair Publications

To see our complete catalog or to order, please write

Perfect Pair Publications
Post Office Box 27041
Knoxville, TN 37927

AN EMOTIONAL HOMICIDE

FIRST EDITON

LORENZO ANDREWS

Perfect Pair Publications, ™ LLC
2025

Welcome to
Perfect Pair Publications

Perfect Pair Publications is an independent publishing company that works with modern talented innovative authors and storytellers.

Our mission is to publish exciting books and make them accessible to the broadest possible audience.

Our focus is to develop authors, help them reach their dreams, and better serve authors and readers than they are supported now. We will focus equal attention on the performance of authors' work after publication, providing them with unparalleled marketing support.

In short, we will offer a personal service and wide dissemination for authors, coupled with the best possible experience for readers.

The vision of Perfect Pair Publications is to inspire excellence and innovation in the selection and presentation of authors.

Our values are excellence, openness, collaboration, innovation, and care. We will offer our authors the traditional publisher experience they value (high quality editorial support and production standards), together with the benefits of unrestricted access to their work. We will build deeply supportive relationships with our authors, helping to curate their work to the highest standard and offering them innovative choices on formats and presentation.

We will work quickly and responsively making best use of technology to increase workflow efficiencies, reduce costs and improve services for our authors and readers.

Our goal is to provide food for thought while promoting unity, peace and love.

Perfect Pair Publications is more than just a publishing company, it's a movement.

Respectfully,

Bashan "BedStuy" Murchison
CEO / Founder of Perfect Pair Publications
www.perfectpairpublications.com

Published by
Perfect Pair Publications, ™ LLC

Copyright © 2020, Text and any other
Author Created Materials Copyright,
Lorenzo Andrews
Designed Cover by: Perfect Pair Publications

Send comments and inquiries to:
Perfect Pair Publications, ™ LLC

Copyright ©2020 by Lorenzo Andrews

Perfect Pair Publications, ™ LLC books may be purchased in bulk at special discounts for sales promotion, corporate gifts, fund-raising, or prisoner wholesalers. For details, contact the Special Sales Department, Perfect Pair Publications, Post Office Box 27041 Knoxville, TN 37927 or email perfectpairpublications@gmail.com

First Printing: 2025

ISBN :9781971056005

The Library of Congress control number is

2025950577

Perfect Pair Publications
Post Office Box 27041
Knoxville, TN 37927

www.perfectpairpublications.com

www. Facebook. Com/ Perfect Pair Publications

DEDICATION

To my Mother, and Grand Mother who provided me with the gift of life and the desire to use that gift effectively. To my Children for all of your faith, trust, and inspiration,

Perfect Pair
Publications,LLC.

Perfect Pair Publications
Unleash Your Inner Author

Submission Guideline

Submit your completed manuscript to perfectpairpublications@gmail.com
In subject line put your book's title. The manuscript must be in .doc
file and sent as an attachment. Documents should be in Times New
Roman, double spaced and in 12 font size. Also, provide your synopsis
and full contact information. If sending multiple submissions, they
must each be in a separate e-mail. Have a story but no way to send it
electronically?
You can still submit to Perfect Pair Publications.
Send in your completed manuscript, written or typed, to:

Perfect Pair Publications
Submissions Dept
Post Office Box 27041
Knoxville, TN 37927

**We are always looking for authors from all walks of life to have their voices
heard.**
**Very important, please be sure you do not send us the only copy of your
manuscript!**
Must be duplicate
Provide your synopsis and a cover letter containing your full contact
information.

Thank you for considering Perfect Pair Publications.

TABLE OF CONTENTS

PERFECT PAIR
PUBLICATIONS

CHAPTER 1
HOW IT STARTED

There is a beautiful bi racial woman sitting in the car with her brother. The woman's name is Amura and her brother's name is Marquis. Amura looks at the rain hitting the front window of the car. She begins to daydream. She is daydreaming about her and her friends. It is a nice winter day in the park. There is a woman standing with a baby in the carriage next to the pond. Her name is Tasha. There are three women walking together in the park. That being Amura, Tawana, and Spanish Fly. They all have sunglasses and trench coats on. The park is crowded with people and children playing. The three women walk up to her. Amura says, "Is this his baby?" "Yes, it is, I got him to let me bring her cute ass to the park. I just gave her a bottle." Tasha replied. One of the other women pulls out a gun with a silencer out of her pocketbook and points it in the baby carriage. Tawana says, "Sorry baby girl, I have to do it, your daddy fucked up." She shoots the baby in the carriage unto all the bullets are out of the gun. The baby's body is riddled with bullets and blood is all inside the baby carriage. All the women walk away from the baby carriage. Amura comes out of her daydream. Her brother passes her a cigarette. Marquis says, "Amura do you ever think about the time when mommy got killed?" "Yeah, I do, all the time." Amura takes a pull from a cigarette and blows it out. The car gets filled with smoke. She slouches in the car seat. Amura says, "I will never forget when that happened, it has been more than 30 years." She begins to daydream. She daydreams about the setting of the sun and the sound of clapping melodies. There are two little girls playing a clapping game on the roof. They turn to the half-opened door because they hear screams and cries from a woman. The two girls run to the door looking down at the spiral stairwell. The spiral stairwell leads to the door where the voices of two women are talking about the noise that is in the hallway. The women (both women are racially mixed and are lesbians) come out of the apartment with their tee shirts and panties, looking down the stairwell complaining. The cops are struggling with a man out the apartment because of a violent dispute. His girlfriend has a black eye crying. Tammy yells, "Please get him out of here. It is over between us." The boyfriend replied, "Fuck you bitch, I'll be back". The cops are struggling with him down the stairs. The two women standing in front of the apartment door are looking down at the incident. Pricilla says, "Damn I wish they shut the fuck-up with all that noise". Her lesbian lover Candy Slim shouts at the man, "What they need to do is get his ass out of here. I mean his broke ass." The man struggling with the cops looks up at the women going down the stairs. Candy Slim shouts, "Yeah motherfucker, I'm talking to you. Officer, get his ass out of here". Pricilla shouts out sarcastically, "Look here, this broke motherfucker again. I bet that punk slapped her again. That's why I say fuck a man, because with me it isn't even going down like that. They hit you before they hit any of them niggas out there." Candy Slim grabs Pricilla's hand, "Come on baby girl, let's go finish with what we were doing. They look down the stairs. Candy Slim shouts, "Tammy it is going to be all right. Go down to the prescient and press charges against him." Pricilla and Candy Slim walk back inside the apartment; Candy Slim slams the door. Candy Slim turns to lock the door and puts the chain lock on too. Candy Slim says, "Ain't no motherfuckin man coming up in here". Candy Slim and Pricilla walk into the kitchen where an open bottle of liquor and two wineglasses are sitting on the countertop. Pricilla pours the liquor into the two wineglasses. They both pick up their wineglasses and walk out of the kitchen. They walk down the dark hallway to a bedroom sipping the liquor from the glass. Candy Slim is dancing to the music from the bedroom. Music of Curtis Mayfield is heard. "Give me your love". The wall is covered with Black and Latino revolutionists. Candy Slim and Pricilla walk in the room sipping from the liquor from the glass. Candy Slim walks to the radio and turns it louder. Candy Slim dances over to Pricilla and they begin to kiss passionately. Candy Slim stops, she drinks the rest of the liquor from the glass and puts the glass on top of the dresser. Pricilla puts her glass on top of the dresser. Candy Slim takes off her shirt and takes Pricilla's shirt off too. Candy Slim shouts, "That is my song girl, "Give me your love". Candy Slim licks her index finger with a lot of saliva and pinch her nipples and licks Pricilla nipple. Pricilla shakes her head in utter disgust. Pricilla whispers to herself, "Only if she knew that I'm still shooting that shit and fucking her children's father." Candy Slim stops licking Pricilla's nipple and looks at her. Candy Slim shouts, "What you say boo?" Pricilla bellows, "I really need to talk to you". Pricilla stares at Candy Slim. She sighs. Candy Slim walks to the radio to turn the music down. "What's wrong? What's wrong?" Pricilla stares at Candy Slim with tears in her eyes, "I don't think I can do this anymore" Pricilla responds. Outside the apartment building. There are four cop cars in front of the apartment building. The lights are flashing and there are some on lookers seeing what has happened. The cop slams the police car door on the man he and his partner got out of the apartment. The woman who was abused by the man is crying standing in front of the building. The other cop is writing information in his report book. Candy Slim's sister Carmen walks up in front of the building, she kindly walks to Tammy. Carmen says, "What happened to your face". Tammy replied, "He hit me again, but this time I'm making sure he goes to jail". Carmen turns and looks at the man in the cop car. "He's a fucking bum anyway". An officer takes notice what Carmen said to the man in the car. The officer closes his report book. Officer Thomas walks over to Carmen and says, "Don't I know you from somewhere?" Carmen is smiling looking at the officer. Carmen says, "No". Officer Thomas smiles and they hug one another. "I can't believe it is you. You look so beautiful. The woman I had a crush on when I was in high school". Another officer escorts Tammy to one of the cop cars. Back up stairs in the apartment, Candy Slim snarls, "Girl, what the fuck are you trying to spit out to me? You can't do what no more." Pricilla talks while she is crying, "Baby my feeling hasn't been the same and when I felt that I slept with someone else". "You did what?" Candy

Slim replied. Candy Slim slaps Pricilla face repeatedly, very hard. She grabs Priscilla's hair, twisting it in her hand and she pulls her closer. She backs Pricilla to the wall. Candy Slim looks very angry and disgusted, and says, "How could you have done this to me? I was there for you. I gave you emotional comfort. I loved you. I even touched you the way a woman wants to be touched, because I'm a fucking woman. I know how a pussy is supposed to get sucked." Pricilla stretches her arms out protecting herself from getting hit. Tears are flowing down Pricilla's face, she speaks sadly, "Baby girl please don't hurt me." Teardrops fall down Pricilla's and Candy 's face. Candy Slim lets go of Pricilla's hair. Candy Slim is sobbing. "You told me you love me". Tears fall down Candy Slim's face. Pricilla says, "Baby girl please, I never meant to hurt you". Candy Slim replies, "I left that no good nigga for you." She grabs the pocket book off of the table and shakes everything out of it to the floor. Lipstick, money, identification, a small bag of heroin, and a heroin needle fall out of the bag. Candy Slim shouts, "You told me that you stop shooting up over year ago. You junkie bitch." The sound of children talking. There are two children (boy and girl) standing by the room door entrance. Their names are Marquis and Amura. The little girl Amura asked her mother Candy Slim, "Mommy,

mommy why are you crying." Candy Slim turns to her children. "Mommy is alright." Pricilla looks at the children then at Candy Slim, "Candy, I'm sorry girl, I'm sorry". Candy Slim shouts to her children, "Y'all go and wake your older brother up so he can go to the bathroom". The children run to their room. Candy Slim and Pricilla can be heard. Candy Slim is cursing and arguing, and Pricilla crying. Amura shakes her brother in the bed while Marquis watches. O's face is never shown. Marquis says, "Come on, you got to go the bathroom. Wake up, mommy want you to go to the bathroom." Candy Slim's voice can be heard in her children's room. "Bitch are you crazy". O wakes up and gets out of the bed to walk to the bathroom. O says, "What is mommy arguing about now? Come on, y'all walk me to the bathroom. I'm scared." Amura replies, "Why are you scared, and you are the oldest?" Candy Slim walks pass the kids room and she shouts, "Go your ass to the bathroom and go back to sleep, all of you." Omar walks out of the room to go to the bathroom. The bathroom is right next to the bedroom. Candy Slim walks in the kitchen and grabs the bottle of liquor. Candy Slim then walks over to the kitchen draw quietly. She opens draw and she gets an ice pick. She takes the ice pick and puts it in back of her thong. The ice pick is down the crack of her sexy ass. She walks out of the kitchen down the hallway.

The children walk out of the bathroom to go into the room. Candy Slim walks down the hallway drinking from the bottle and stops in front of the children's room. She tells the kids, "Go your asses to bed, and O you better not pee in the bed." She closes the door and turns the key that is in the lock. The children are locked in the room. Outside the apartment, Candy Slim's sister Carmen and the cop are walking up the stairs in the apartment building. They are three flights away from the apartment. Carmen says to the cop, "I live three more flights, so what time are you getting off", she asks the Officer Thomas. Back inside the apartment, Pricilla is in the room crying with her back to the wall. Candy Slim drinks from the bottle of liquor. She puts the bottle of liquor on the dresser and walks over to Pricilla. Candy Slim is angry, she says, "So you took my kindness for a weakness. This is your pay back to me. Didn't I fuck you good enough?" Pricilla wipes the tears from her face and shouts, "Your kindness for a weakness, you beat my fucking ass every other day. I'm tired of this fucking relationship. I'm leaving you." Candy Slim responds, "What"? Candy Slims kisses Pricilla. Pricilla moves her face. "You love me right". Pricilla's looks Candy Slim in the eyes and says, "I'm pregnant, and it's by your kid's father." Candy Slim is shocked, "I left him for you bitch and you are having his baby, you no good motherfucker!" Candy Slim says furiouly. Candy Slim pulls out the ice pick from the crack of her ass and stabs Pricilla in the stomach and over here body with the ice pick like a maniac, stabbing here repeatedly. Candy Slim is in rage. Candy Slim says repeatedly, "How could you have done this to me?" Pricilla screams are thunderous with her last bit of life as the ice pick goes inside and out of her body. Outside the apartment, Carmen and the officer hear Pricilla screaming. They are standing in front of the apartment door. Carmen is trying to find her keys. Carmen yells, "My sister and her kids are in there." She is checking her pockets, and her pocketbook for the keys. Inside the apartment, Pricilla falls to the floor. Pricilla is repeatedly stabbed by Candy Slim with the ice pick. Outside the apartment the officer pulls out his gun, and he kicks the door in, breaking the lock and the chain. They both ran into the apartment. They investigate the kitchen then they follow the sound of the voice. Carmen yells, "It's coming from the back." The officer and Carmen run down the apartment hallway. They make a left turn, and the officer see's Candy Slim stabbing Pricilla to death, blood is all over her. Candy Slim drops the ice pick. "Carmen screams, "Oh my God, where are the kids" The children bang on the door crying and screaming for their mother. They want to get out of the room. Carmen stops and unlocks the lock on the door and opens the door. The children try to run out but Carmen pushes them back into the room. The officer slows down walking down the hallway into the room with his gun drawn. Inside the room, blood is all over Pricilla's body. Her breast and stomach have holes from the ice pick. Pricilla's last thoughts before she dies. She looks at Candy Slim. Pricilla murmurs in a soft voice, "You killed my baby. Please Lord, don't let me die. I have a minute to pray and a second to die. All my life I've seen heartache and pain. I thought I could have been loved, I must have been insane, making love to woman, being romanced by a man. This is one race I have lost again. I have a minute to pray and a second to die." The life has left Pricilla's body. Pricilla is dead. Blood is all over Candy Slim breast and hands. She has an unwelcoming look. She looks like the lady from in the movie "Carrie". The officer is in shock to see what he is seeing. Candy Slim noticed that the officer and her sister were in the room. She picks the ice pick off of the floor. The officer has his gun pointed at Candy Slim. Carmen is shocked that her sister has stabbed Pricilla to death. Officer Thomas yells, "Put that weapon down now". Candy Slim stands up with the ice pick in her hand. Blood is all over her naked body. Carmen yells, "Candy put that fucking ice pick down". I can't believe you did

AN EMOTIONAL HOMICIDE

this shit. I told you to leave that bitch alone." The children are crying and screaming for their mother. And you locked the fucking kids in the room for this shit. Officer Thomas yells, "Put the weapon down now." The children try to run out but Carmen pushes them back into the room. Candy Slim backs away from Pricilla's body. The officer is walking toward her. The officer has his gun drawn pointed at Candy Slim. Officer Thomas yells, "Put the weapon down and put your hands up." Candy Slim barks, "Fuck You!" Carmen shouts, "What have you just done Candy?" Candy Slim replies, "I just stabbed this bitch with this ice pick, she was fucking my kid's father. I left him for her". She holds the ice pick up. "And I'm going to stick this in his throat if he doesn't stop aiming that gun at my fucking face". Candy Slim runs to the officer with the ice pick making an attempt to kill. Carmen yells, "No, no Candy no. The officer shoots Candy Slim in the chest. Candy Slim falls to the floor. The officer stands in disbelief. Carmen runs to her sister crying. The blood flows from Candy Slim chest. Carmen bends down on the floor hugging Candy Slim. She rests Candy Slim's head on her lap. Her hands and clothing are covered with her sister's blood. Carmen speaks to her dead sister. She cries and mutters, "Damn girl, you done did it this time. If only you could see yourself dead. You would be crying like me." Marquis runs past the cop to his aunt and his dead

11

mother. Marquis says, "Auntie, what happen to my mommy?" Carmen replies, "Marquis move." She pushes him away, knocking him down to the floor. "Baby I'm sorry. Get up and go over there with your sister and brother." Marquis gets up from the floor, and he is looking at the syringe that is on the floor. He stares at the needle, and he reaches to pick it up. "Leave that on the floor baby. Don't touch it." Marquis turns away and walks over to his brother and sister who are crying. The officer reaches for his radio. Officer Thomas speaks into the police radio, "Code 3 domestic violence, suspect approached by officer, attacked by suspect with an ice pick, suspect shot by officer. Suspect also murdered a female with an ice pick." Voice from radio, "10-4." Carmen lays her sister back on the floor. Carmen stands up and tells the children to go into the room. The children stand looking. The children are standing next to one another Amura is in full light, Marquis is in half-light, and O's face is shaped in the darkness, never being seen. The sound of a fire truck's siren gets the attention of the children. They all turn their heads in the same direction. A fire truck rides by blowing the horn and the lights flashing. Amura comes out of her daydream. She is looking at the rear-view mirror. The car behind flicks the headlights off and on. Amura is hearing her name being called by her brother Marquis. "Amura, Amura, Amura." Amura responds, "What motherfucker? You are one sick bastard." "What are you talking about?" Amura stares at Marquis and says, "Yeah, you know when mommy died, I seen you looking at the needle that was on the floor. Now you stick it in your arms." Marquis replies, "Your point is!" Amura is looking at Marquis holding a syringe in his hand. He reaches for his cigarette in the ash tray. He sucks the smoke from the cigarette and blows it in her face. Amura gets out of the car. She has on a trench coat. She walks to the trunk of the car. Three women get out of the car that is parked behind Amura and Marquis. They are sexy women. Spanish Fly who is Latino American, Tasha who is a blonde hair blue eye Russian- American, Tawana and Black American. They all walk over to Amura, giving her a kiss on the lips. Amura says, "It is about time you bitches got here. One of the females respond. Tawana says, "We all went to get our hair done." Tasha speaks with her Russian accent, "These braids are so tight." Tasha rubs her head. Amura sticks her key inside the lock to open the trunk. She reaches for a gun. Amura says, "Fly, did you bring the lighter fluid?" Spanish Fly responds, "Yes I did." Amura gets the gun out of the trunk and puts the gun on her waistline, and she reaches back in the trunk for 5 pairs of leather gloves. She gives Tasha, Spanish Fly, and Tawana each a pair of gloves. She slams the trunk shut. Marquis gets out of the car slamming the door. He throws his cigarette on the ground. Amura passes Marquis a pair of gloves. Everybody put their gloves on. Marquis says, "Give me an hour and I will have that bitch cloths off. I'm going to get that bitch doped up. I got some good shit from Amsterdam. She likes for me to shoot that shit between her toes and in her nipples. She is a very freaky bitch, thanks to me." He points to himself. He then points to the ladies, "So I'll be seeing you bitches up stairs."

★★★

One hour later

Marquis is in the room squeezing the baby oil all over the woman's naked body. The gun that is on his waistline can be seen. He rubs the baby oil on her body from head to her breast, then to her toes. He licks her toes. The room has mirrors on the ceiling. Marquis looks at the syringe on the nightstand through the corner of his eye. He reaches for the syringe. He presses the top of the syringe, leaking some of the heroin out. The woman arches her feet, stretching her toes apart. Marquis says, "Which one you want it in? Right or the left." Kima responds, "It doesn't matter. Just give me a little for now. Kima begins to squeeze her nipples. Marquis sticks the needle between her toes. He sucks her toes. She begins to yearn. Pitching her nipples harder, pulling and shaking her breast. She is looking at herself in the mirror. A knock on the door gets Marquis attention. Marquis turns his head, and then he looks back at Kima. He climbs on Kima and licks her lips. He gets off of her to walk out of the room to open the door. Amura, Tawana, Tasha, and Spanish Fly are standing at the apartment door knocking. Amura says, "How much did you pay to get your hair done Tasha?" Amura looks at Tasha and Spanish Fly's hair. Spanish Fly's hair is straight down passing her shoulder. And Tasha with French braids, Tawana has dreadlocks. Amura begins to rub Tasha's hair. Tasha moves her head. Tasha says, "Can't touch this, you know that M.C. Hammer song." Amura shakes her head and smiles. Marquis opens the door and speaks. "Right on time ladies. She's in the room zoned out masturbating. She's in the room putting her fingers in her asshole." Marquis moves from the door. The ladies walk inside the apartment behind Marquis. Tawana closes the door. They are walking down the apartment hallway. The apartment is dim. Spanish Fly says, "What is in here to eat?" Marquis replies, "Didn't you go to the cuche fritos? Marquis and Spanish Fly reach for their guns from their waste line. They both point their guns in the same direction at one another. Amura reacts, "Stop that tit for tat shit, and come on." They both put

15

their guns away. They all walk into the room to see Kima squeezing her nipple, and sucking her index finger, moaning. Amura walks past everybody and slaps Kima in the face. Kima is frantic. She comes out of her sexual ecstasy, but she is still high from the heroin injection. Kima studiers, "What the fuck is going on? Marquis, why is your sister doing this to me? I never did anything to her." Kima tries to block Amura's slaps. All of the women begin to hit Kima. Tasha and Marquis hold her arms down to the bed. Tawana takes duct tape out her coat pocket and breaks apiece off and puts it on Kima's mouth. Kima is silent trying her best to scream. Tawana stares at Spanish Fly. Tawana says, "Fly, Amura, put that bitch legs together." Spanish Fly holds one of her legs. And Amura grabs the other one. Tawana wraps the duct tape around Kima's ankles. Kima's legs are stuck together. Tawana walks over to Tasha and wraps the duct tape to Kima's wrists to the bedpost. Then she walks around the bed to Marquis and duck tapes the other wrist to the bedpost. Marquis is looking at Kima. Her tears flow from her eyes down her face with mascara. Kima's arms are spread apart like the crucifix. Spanish Fly takes lighter fluid out of her coat pocket and squeezes it all over Kima's body. Kima is trying to scream for her dear life. Spanish Fly squeezes it to the last drops, shaking the bottle over

Kima's body. Amura walks over and bends over to whisper in Kima's ear. "You know what you did to my brother. Now you are going to suffer." Amura licks Kima in her face, then spits in her face. Everyone in the room walks out. Marquis slides all the heroin and the paraphernalia (syringe, spoon, cotton balls and the heroin) off of the table into a bag. Tawana stops and turns around. Tawana shouts, "Tell God I said hi or if you are going to hell, blow the devil a kiss for me." Tawana leaves out of the room. Amura goes into her pants pocket for matches. She lights the match and throws it on Kima's body. Kima's body is in flames. Amura stands there and watches, and then she leaves the room. Kima is watching herself burn in the mirrors hanging from the wall. Her body is jumping in the bed like a fish out of water.

CHAPTER 2

THE ARRIVAL

An airplane has just landed at Kennedy Airport in New York City. People are getting their luggage leaving the plane. There is one female with headphones on sleeping in the chair. The female name is Precious Jewell. She has a Gucci bag sitting on her lap. She does not know that the flight is over. A flight attendant comes over to shake the female so she can wake up. The flight attendant shoves her shoulder. The flight attendant says, "Ma'am, ma'am, the flight is over." The flight attendant is getting frustrated. She takes a deep breath. "Excuse me, miss, miss. Hello, hello." The woman wakes up and takes off her headphones. Precious Jewell shouts, "What? What the hell do you want? Wasn't I sleeping?" The flight attendant replies, "The flight is over." Precious Jewell shakes her head. "I'm sorry. She is looking confused getting her belongings. "I'm just so very tired." The flight attendant smiles, "It's okay ma'am really." Precious Jewell replies, "Where do I exit?" The flight attendant points to the door with a smile. "The same way you came in ma'am." Precious Jewell gets her bag and exits the plane. The flight attendant shakes her head, "What a stupid bitch." Precious Jewell walks through the crowded terminal to a concession stand looking at the magazines. She picks up a newspaper. The newspaper has on the front cover, "Female Found In Blazing Fire Ducked Taped To The Bed". Also on the front cover are two men carrying out a dead body in the body bag. She puts the paper down. She walks over to the cargo area looking for her bag to come down the conveyer belt. She sees her duffle bag and picks it up. She puts the bag around her body. Precious Jewell is making her way out of the terminal through the doors. She walks through the sliding doors with her duffle bag, then to the curb to wave for a cab. A cab pulls over. She drops her bag on the ground. The cab driver opens the trunk lock from inside the car. The trunk opens halfway. The cab driver looks at Precious Jewell. Precious Jewell looks at the cab driver. Precious Jewell says, "I know you are going to get the hell out and put my bag in the trunk." The African cab driver shouts, "You must be crazy, my back hurts." Precious Jewell shouts back, "Get your ass out of here, and put my fucking bag in the trunk before I report your ass. The cab driver shakes his head and bellows, "You fucking lazy Americans." Especially you Black Americans." The African cab driver gets out of the car. He grabs the bag off of the ground and throws her bag in the trunk. He then slams the trunk looking at Precious Jewell. Precious Jewell's says with smile, "I'm not scared of you." She opens the cab door and gets in the back seat. She slams the door. The cab driver gets into the cab, and he slams the door. Precious Jewell is sitting in the back seat looking at the cab driver and the cab driver is looking back at Precious Jewell. The cab driver asks, "So where are we headed?" "111th and Lexington." The cab driver shouts, "Miss, you pay me now. The last time I went over there, I got beaten with a garbage can lit. That's why my back is hurting." He points at Precious Jewell. "So, you pay me now. Precious Jewell shouts back, "What?" "Yes, pay me now, or out you go." Precious Jewell says furiously, "Oh no you won't put my shit and me in the street." Precious Jewell is getting angry. The cab drivers grabs a small bat with nails in it, "Oh yeah, try me lady". Precious Jewell looks at the bat and the cab driver. "Ain't this a bitch, how much." "It will cost you 35 dollars." Precious Jewell digs in her pocketbook and pulls out two 20-dollar bills. She passes it to the cab driver. "Here keep the change." The cab driver replies, "Yes, I am, I was going to keep the change anyway. The cab driver presses the gas pedal and the force from the car makes Precious Jewell fall back in the back seat. They drive out of the airport. Precious Jewell is in the back of the cab looking for something in her pocketbook. The cab driver is paying attention to the road. He's driving on the freeway. Precious Jewell finds what she is looking for. She pulls out a CD. Precious asks pleasantly, "Could you play this? It is Isaac Hayes." "I love his music." The cab driver reaches for the CD and puts it in. The music plays the song "Don't Go". Precious Jewell goes in her pocketbook and pulls out a marijuana joint, and a lighter. She puts the joint in her mouth, then she lights it. She inhales, and then she coughs. The cab driver is looking at her through the rear-view mirror. The cab driver says, "You know that you're not supposed to be smoking that shit in here. Can I take a few pulls?" Precious Jewell coughs from her inhaling the smoke. The smoke fills the air. "I'll pass it to you." Precious Jewell reaches back in her bag and pulls out an envelope. She takes a letter out of the envelope. She unfolds the letter and reads it. She takes another pull from the joint. She coughs harder than before. Her eyes are glossy. "Damn this is some good shit. Here take it." She passes the marijuana to the cab driver. He reaches for it and he inhales the smoke from the joint. The cab driver coughs very hard. The cab driver says, "Damn this is some good shit." Precious Jewell reads the letter. It says, "Dear Precious, It has been 12 years since I seen you. I'm not the one for words, so get your ass on an airplane and come stay with your cousin for a while. Love Sheeka". Precious Jewell relaxes in the back seat. She takes a deep breath and closes her eyes from her being high. She opens her eyes. She sees the street number 111th. She shouts, "That's the block right there, slow down. 111th and Lexington." The cab driver slows down and parks the car. The cab driver pops the trunk open, and he quickly gets out of the cab to get the bag from the trunk. "Yo, what's the fucking hurry? Precious Jewell grabs her Gucci bag and gets out of the car. Precious Jewell slams the door; she walks to the back of the car. He reaches for her bag out of the trunk and throws it on the ground. "What the fuck is your problem and give me back my CD." He says, "I must go from here, and I'm keeping the CD." The cab driver slams the trunk, and he gets in his cab and speeds off. The smoke from the tires fills the air. Precious Jewell is coughing, "Ain't this something?" She coughs covering her nose and mouth with one hand and she sticks her middle finger up with the other. Precious Jewell picks her bag off of the ground. She says to herself, "Let me find this building." "She walks on the sidewalk looking for the number to the building dropping her bag. "23-11, 23-11 right here." She walks closer to the building. "Damn, Sheeka said she lived on the 4th floor." Precious Jewell looks up at the apartment building. She yells, "Sheeka, Sheeka, Sheeka." Precious Jewell paces the pavement looking up at the apartment building dropping her bag. Sheeka looks out of the window and yells. "Is that my baby girl? Precious Jewell that's you. I'm coming down." Sheeka sticks her head back in the window. She is coming down to greet Precious Jewell. Precious Jewell says to herself, "About time. Shit, I thought she was never going to answer. Damn. Fucking with my nerves already." There are two young ladies walking past looking at Precious Jewell. Precious Jewell and the ladies make eye contact. "I'm not going to fuck your man, so keep it moving." Precious Jewell goes inside her pocketbook and pulls out a box cutter. "Bitch I'll cut your face, then your man will have a reason to fuck me. He wouldn't want to look in your fucked up face." Sheeka comes through the building door. The two women walk away. Sheeka says, "Precious please, you just got here, starting shit already. I haven't seen you in years and you got the same attitude. Stink!" Precious rolls her eyes at Sheeka. Sheeka snatches the bag off the pavement. "Come on upstairs." Precious Jewell speaks with an attitude, "I'm not a little child anymore. I got hairs on my pussy. I bleed." "O.K. your pussy got hair on it, I just hope you don't have crabs." Sheeka and

Precious Jewell smile at one another. Sheeka drops the bag on the floor. "Baby girl give me a hug." They both hug one another. "I miss you." Precious Jewell starts to cry. "Sheeka that so-called man, that motherfucker abused me. He beat me with the heel of his shoe; he beat me with a belt like I was his fucking child. He beat me with a coat hanger like I was a whore on the street Sheeka, on the day of my mother's funeral. I miss my mommy." Sheeka responds, "I know baby girl, I miss her too. Come on, let's go upstairs so you can relax. Come on baby girl, dry your eyes." Sheeka picks Precious Jewell's bag off of the ground. They both walk into the building to go up stairs. Precious Jewell wipes the tears from her face. They walk up to the fourth floor to Sheeka's apartment. Apartment 4a. Sheeka and Precious Jewell walk into the apartment. Sheeka closes the door. "Damn Sheeka. I like this." Precious Jewell walks into the living room. She sees a very big T.V, a very big black leather couch with nightstands with white lamps, and a stereo system with hundreds of CD's. Sheeka puts Precious Jewell bag down on the floor and walks up to Precious Jewell. "You like it. I had a little money saved and I paid the rent for the next three years. Whatever is mine, it is yours." Precious Jewell looks at the living room in ore. "I know you love to party. We're going to a club tonight. Fuck being tired." Precious Jewell responds, "Since you said that I'm wide-awake." Sheeka replied, I just took a shower and I know your pussy is stinking. So, you go on and get in the shower. We are going to a club tonight." Sheeka points to the shower. "There is a blue rag hanging up." Precious Jewell walks toward the bathroom. "All right, you don't have to tell me twice." She takes off her shirt. She doesn't have a bra on, so her breast is shown. Then she takes off her shoes, then her pants. She walks in the red and blue lighten bathroom. She closes the door. Sheeka shouts, "You better pick your shit up when you come out." Incents are burning in the bathroom. Precious Jewell reaches to turn on the water on for the shower. She gets it to the right temperature. She takes off her panties, and then she steps in looking at the shower. The water is splashing on her body. The red and blue lights are reflecting off her glossy watered body.

Two hours later.

The sound of thunder and rain is hitting the windowpane. Precious Jewell and Sheeka are looking at their selves in the mirror-putting make- up on. They're both dressed sexy with high heels showing their beautiful feet. Sheeka says, "I better bring an umbrella. "Come on girl, it is going to be a dance contest tonight. I heard this from one of my friends, who was in jail with me." Her cousin is dancing tonight. So let's go. I want to see some old foes of mine. We better bring our jackets. I have two in the closet." Sheeka walks over to the closet and get two leather jackets. Sheeka passes Precious Jewell one of the jackets. They both put the jackets on. Precious Jewell says, "I'm ready girl. Damn, don't I look good? Oops, I almost forgot, I need my blade." "Let's go." Sheeka tells Precious Jewell. Sheeka and Precious Jewell walk out of the room. Sheeka then Precious Jewell walks out of the apartment. Precious Jewell slams the apartment door, and it makes a loud echo in the hallway. Sheeka turns around in disgust. Sheeka shouts, "Did you have to slam the fucking door like that?" Precious Jewell responds, "I'm making sure that the door is lock, it is a slam lock, right." "Don't be slamming my fucking door like that." They both walk down the spiral staircase. Sheeka sighs, "I forgot the umbrellas. Fuck it." Sheeka and Precious Jewell walks out of the building. It is raining lightly. They both walk to the curb to hail down a cab. A cab pulls over, and they both get in. They are on their way to the club. In an alley way behind a club. Smoke fills the air. Amura, Spanish Fly, Tawana, and Tasha are all smoking marijuana in the parked car in the alleyway. They are all dressed like they are in the 70's. Amura, "I'm going to go speak with Bigtime and Marquis. Spanish Fly coughs from her inhaling the marijuana. Tasha says, "This is that head banging boogie. Little girls like you need not to apply. Tasha takes another pull from the joint. Spanish Fly looks at Amura. Tell your brother we got that bitch real good. Spanish Fly coughs while she is speaking. That will send a message to all our competition and even the people who works for us that we are not to be fucked with. The women get out of the car. The women are walking to the entrance in back of the club. Amura is walking through the alley to go to the street. The street is lit up from the lights that are in front of the club displaying the name of the club, "Ballroom". There are people standing outside on line to get in the club. Amura walks across the street to the parked car. There are two men sitting in the car, one in the driver's seat, and the other in the passenger seat. Amura opens the car door. Amura gets in the back seat of the car. Marquis and Bigtime sits in the front of the car. Bigtime's face is not shown. He is in the shadow. The sound of rain hitting the car. The man in the driver's seat is coughing. Marquis turns around in the front seat. Marquis turns to speak to his sister, "What up sis?" Bigtime the man in the driver's seat lights his cigarette. The smoke from the cigarette gets thick in the air. He coughs. Bigtime speaks with a sore throat. "Did you and the ladies handle that for me?" Amura replies, "We torched that bitch." "Good." Bigtime is in shadow never seeing his face, only the shape of his head. "Someone in the crew ran their mouth about how we do things. You know our shit is straight gangsta shit. I think it was your little pussycat. Amura take care of all the weak links in the chain. With one weak link, the chain will never hold." Amura responds, "I'll handle that." Marquis turns his head looking out the window. He is shocked at what he has seen. He is looking out the window at Sheeka and Precious Jewell getting out of the cab in the rain. Marquis is looking in the direction of the club, "Yo, now ain't that something. When did she come home?" Bigtime and Amura turn their heads to see whom Marquis is talking about. They see Sheeka and Precious Jewell. "Amura that's Sheeka, damn that bitch went to jail for at least 7 years. Hard." Marquis conveys to Sheeka. Bigtime is looking at Amura through the rear-view mirror. He has glasses on (tinted). Amura is looking out the car window. Bigtime says, "It was either her or you Amura." Amura replies, "So we saw the outcome. I know she is mad, but that is the rules of the game. Either you get rich, go to jail, or get buried in the ground. At least she got one out of the three." Marquis is in ore to what he seeing, "Who is the find young lady with her?" Precious Jewell and Sheeka are walking to the entrance of the club. Precious Jewell turns around and looks in the direction of the car before she walks in the club. Amura says, "I would love to fuck her. I'll put my tongue all in her ass." Marquis turns around to Amura, "O.K. we will each have a chance when we get into the club, I bet I'll get her strung out on heroin." Amura replies, "O.K. we will each have a chance when we get inside." Marquis laughs and says, "That's a deal, and we have a third-party witness. Bigtime's right glass lens is nodding up and down in the rear-view mirror. Bigtime says, "That's right." Marquis looks back at his sister and says, "You know what, I find it so ironic that you through dirt on me about my drug habit. But I see that you have some habits of your on. I see you really like women. Just like mommy." Amura replies, "A man can't do shit for me. I remember the first time I did it. I didn't like it then and I know I wound like it now. A woman knows how a woman should be treated, because she is a woman. Women have the same emotions, plus a woman know how a woman's pussy is supposed be sucked. I can't help if there is an attraction. I was born this way." Marquis says sarcastically, "Well, I know how I like my dick sucked and you don't see me wanting no man to suck my dick. And on that note", Marquis turns to Bigtime, "Bigtime it is always a pleasure." Bigtime makes known, "Tell the girls I said hello." I got to catch my flight to L.A., a motherfucker came up short about 200,000 dollars again, what is up with this $200,000 coming up short thing." Bigtime looks at his watch. He coughs. "Damn, I got to make this flight." Amura says, "See you later, I'll tell the girls you said hello. Bigtime asks, "Are we making money in that fucking club?" Amura and Marquis got out of the car. Amura shouts, "What the fuck you think?" Marquis and Amura closes the car door. The car pulls off. Amura and Marquis walk across the street toward the club. A car speeds by them. Marquis and Amura walk across the street to the club. They walk pass all the security. All of the security smiles and greetings at the both of them as they walk into the club. People are in the club dancing and sitting down listening to the loud music. The music that is playing is Run-DMC "King Of Rock". People are sitting at the bar drinking and smoking. Amura and Marquis walk into the club and sees Sheeka and Precious Jewell sitting at the bar. Amura takes off her coat. A female employee walks over and Amura passes her the coat to her and kisses the employee on the lips. Precious Jewell and Sheeka are sitting at the bar. Sheeka says, "I got to go to the bathroom." Order the drinks Precious, I'll be right back. Precious Jewell answers back, "What drink you want?" "Absolute and cranberry juice." Amura and Marquis are looking at Sheeka and Precious Jewell sitting at the bar.

PERFECT PAIR PUBLICATIONS....

"Amura says to Marquis, "There she goes you go kick your tired ass game while I talk to Sheeka." Sheeka walks away from the bar. Marquis responds, "We will see." He licks his index finger and straightens out his eyebrow. Amura barks, "Hurry up!" Amura walks through the crowd to meet with Sheeka. Sheeka comes out of the huge crowd. Sheeka sees Amura and they make eye contact. Then they walk toward one another. Marquis can be seen right behind Sheeka, sitting at the bar with Precious Jewell. Sheeka and Amura give each other a kiss on the lips. Amura says, "How have you been Sheeka?" Sheeka bellows, "It's so funny how you would ask me some shit like that?" Amura says, "Sheeka, I know how you feel." Sheeka holler, "Bitch, no you don't know how I feel. Seven fucking years, hard for your ass. And you only did one." Sheeka begins to count her fingers. "One, Two, Three, Four, Five, Six, you know what the fuck I mean." Marquis leaves away from the bar with Precious Jewell. It catches Amura's attention. Amura, "I really did miss you Sheeka, especially all the good times we had, you know." Sheeka storms back to say, "Well, I hate to cut the conversation short, but I got to use the bathroom. And I see you did a nice fucking job with this place. I remember when it first opened up. Seven fucking years ago." Sheeka walks away bumping Amura. Amura turns looking at Sheeka. Amura says jokingly, "Can I have a kiss boo? See you later, you

31

should stop by one day." Sheeka looks at Amura shaking her head. Amura grins and walks toward the bar. Precious Jewell gets up from the bar with the drinks. Amura brushes up against Precious Jewell. Amura is looking at Precious Jewell licking her lips. Sheeka comes out of the bathroom. Sheeka sees Precious Jewell walking through the crowd and a man gets a drink thrown in his face by a woman. Precious Jewell passes Sheeka her drink. The crowd of people forms a circle around two girls. The two girls are competing against one another in dancing. One of the dancers acts like they have a gun with their hands and makes a jester like she is shooting a gun. The DJ who is playing the music ends the song with a loud gunshot sound, Boom!

Early the next morning.

Precious Jewell and Skeeka are in the bed sleeping. Precious Jewell is having a dream. She is in a room lit with black candles. Precious Jewell is walking into the room slowly. There is a woman lying in the bed. The woman's face is in darkness. The woman that is lying in the bed is Amura. Amura says, "Who do you expect?" She leans forward in the bed to the light. "Shaquille O'Neil." The sound of a fire truck roaring down the street. It gets

Precious Jewell's attention. She turns her head. Precious Jewell turns around and sees a man in shadow swinging a knife. Precious Jewell wakes up out of her dream from the sound of a fire truck roaring down the street. She is lying in the bed with her cousin Sheeka. Sheeka body lies on her left side not in view of Precious Jewell. They both have on a tee shirt and panties on. Precious Jewell turns over to Sheeka. Precious Jewell says, "Sheeka get up. Precious Jewell shakes Sheeka. Sheeka responds, "I'm up already." "Give me a cigarette Sheeka." "My cigarettes are on the dresser." Precious Jewell gets up to walk over to the dresser to get a cigarette out of the pack. Get me one too. Precious Jewell gets Sheeka a cigarette also. She lights both the cigarettes with the lighter that is on the dresser. Precious Jewell puts both of the cigarettes in her mouth and lights them both. Precious Jewell drops the lighter on the dresser and hops on it. "What is the deal with you taking me to that club last night? It sure was a lot of lesbians in that club. But I still had a good time." Sheeka gets out of the bed and walks over to Precious Jewell to get her cigarettes. Precious Jewell inhales the smoke from both of the cigarettes. Sheeka takes one of them out of her mouth. Then she begins to smoke. She inhales, and then she exhales the smoke in the air. "I didn't sleep at all." Precious Jewell says, "Why is that Sheeka?" Sheeka responds, "I seen some one last night

33

that I've had not seen in a long time. My mine is blown away on how Amura not even giving a fuck." Sheeka inhales the smoke deeply and blows out a lot of smoke. "The only thing I need is some coffee and I'm straight. A caffeine and nicotine high." Precious Jewell responds, "All right, now back to whom you saw last night at the club. By the way, who was that lady you were talking to last night? Sheeka says, "That's Amura. That bitch and I got issues." Sheeka gets angry and paces the floor back and forth. She is inhaling and exhaling from the cigarette. Sheeka what is wrong with you?" Precious asks. "That bitch Amura! I went down for that bitch, Precious. I spent 7 years in jail for her. I heard in jail, someone was working to get her off the charges from the time the FEDS ran up in that club we were in." Precious Jewell inhales and exhales the smoke from the cigarette. Precious Jewell says, "That woman walked up to me and rubbed up against me. Sheeka says, "We use to fuck, but let me tell you, Precious, Amura is bad people. Don't fuck with her O. K. I did 7 years in jail for her. Precious Jewell" "Damn, I didn't know you went that way. So that's why you went to jail." Sheeka replies, "That's not important, just stay away from her." Precious Jewell, "Please, I'm not thinking about her. Besides, I'm not a little girl anymore." Precious Jewell hops off of the dresser draw, and then she walks over to the window.

AN EMOTIONAL HOMICIDE

Precious Jewell says, "You know what, it seems like a cool place." She plucks the cigarette out of the window. Sheeka replies, "Yeah Precious, be careful baby girl, things done change on this side." Sheeka walks out of the room, and she returns with a broom and passes it to Precious Jewell. Sheeka puts the cigarette out in the ash tray that is on the dresser. "Clean up Precious. And one more thing miss hot ass, if you plan on going out there to fuck, don't come in this house with a swollen pussy and empty pockets.

Across Town At Amura's House

There are two women sleeping in bed together. They are sleeping in a lavish perch room. Amura and Veryfine are sleeping in the bed together under the sheets. A knock on the door (Boom, Boom, Boom). Amura and Veryfine wake up from the knocking. Veryfine says, "Baby I know you are going to get the door." Amura shouts, "Who the fuck is it knocking at my door?" Amura reaches between the nightstand and the bed to grab a baseball bat that got nails in it. She gets out of the bed to walk to the door. She has on her thong and bra on. Marquis is standing outside Amura's apartment banging on the door. Amura is walking down the hallway to the door. Amura shouts, "Who the hell is it?" Marquis replies, "It's Marquis. "What the hell you want?" Open the motherfuckin' door before I open it for you." Amura says, "What's the password?" Amura unlocks the door. Marquis is standing at the door. He has a 1970's look leather coat and glasses. Marquis replies, "The password is my dick in your girl's mouth. Bitch open the door, I wanna get high." "I hope it's some herb." Amura opens the door and Marquis walks inside the apartment. Amura closes the door. They both walk down the hallway into Amura's bedroom. Amura's girlfriend Veryfine is lying in the bed smoking a cigarette with sheets wrap up on her. Amura and Marquis walk into the room. Amura puts the bat between the nightstand, and the bed gets back in bed with her girlfriend. Veryfine passes her the cigarette and kisses her on the lips. Amura says, "Good morning." Marquis is standing watching the both of them. Marquis says, "Amura, I'm feeling kind of horny, you think your girl can hit me off." Amura, replies, "You better take your ass to the crack house around the corner." Marquis takes his jacket off. He has on a short sleeve shirt. He pulls out a syringe and a zip lock bag of heroin out of his jacket and throughs it on Amura's bed. He takes his glasses off and drops it on the bed. Marquis says, "I saw you talking to Sheeka last night. What is going on with her?" "She needs to use her anger control." Marquis says, "I wouldn't blame Sheeka for being mad.

She did do 7 years in jail for you. You should've tried harder to get her an appeal or something." Amura says, "Fuck Sheeka! What did you say to that little sweetheart? What is her name? Marquis says, "Precious Jewell. I asked her who she was here with, you wouldn't believe it. She's Sheeka's cousin. But don't think about it because she gonna get my loving. Amura says, "Whatever? Oh yeah, Bigtime said to get your shit together because that's bad for business. We got to handle something tonight, so be there at 12:00." Amura and Marquis make eye-to-eye contact. Amura moves her eyes to the left. She is moving them in the direction where Veryfine is lying at. She puts her cigarette out in the ash trey on the nightstand. Marquis, "Cool. You spoke to Bigtime." "Amura Yes I did. He said not to step on the smack too hard. He wants a few people to die of an overdose. Plus he said we are charging 450 a gram." Marquis responds, "He told me that all ready. Shit I have some right here. He looks at Veryfine and licks his lips, "So Veryfine, you feel like being with a man this morning." Veryfine responds, "Leave me alone." Amura says, "Watch your mouth, cause ain't none of my bitches I'm sleeping with fucks with a men. Shit they better not." Marquis looks on the floor and he sees a pair of pants. Amura and Veryfine are looking at him. He takes the belt out of the pants. He ties the belt around his arm very tightly. He picks up the syringe and the heroin off of the bed to go into the kitchen. Marquis walks into the kitchen and turns the stove on. He opens the drawer to get a very big tablespoon. He reaches over to the kitchen sink and turns on the faucet and puts a little bit of water on to the spoon. He reaches inside the zip lock bag and gets a pitch heroin out and puts it in the spoon. Takes the spoon and puts it over the fire and warms the heroin to it boils. He reaches to the cabinet to get a shot glass and puts the heroin in it from the spoon. He then gets the syringe and injects the heroin into the syringe. He looks for a vein in his arm. He fines and open hole in his arm. He ejects the heroin into his vein in his arm. He shakes and he shivers. He then falls on the floor still shivering. His sister Amura walks in the kitchen. She looks at him on the floor. She steps over him and walks to the refrigerator to get some pizza that is cold. She takes a slice and walks right back over him. She stops and turns around and looks. Amura says, " Damn that is some good shit. We're going to make a lot of money. She walks out of the kitchen.

★★★

Back At Sheeka's House.
Sheeka is standing at the door with her clothing and coat on. She opens the door and two plain cloth cops are

standing there. Sheeka says, "Hey, y'all right on time. She turns around she shouts, "Precious, Precious." Precious Jewell comes out of the bathroom. "What's up Sheeka? And who are those people? "It's my parole officer. I violated my parole, so I got to go in for about 8-9 months. After this, I don't owe them any more time. So, take care of my apartment. There are some keys in the room on the dresser. I'll call you." She turns around for the parole officer to put on the handcuffs on. "Sheeka, why didn't you tell me this?" "It just slipped my mind. And stay your ass away from the club." Sheeka replied. The parole officers take Sheeka away. The door closes. "Now what the fuck I'm I going to do? Precious Jewell looks around the apartment. "Go my ass to bed." Precious Jewell walks to the bedroom. She walks in the room and falls in the bed. She looks at the clock. It is 3:30PM. Precious Jewell closes her eyes slowly.

★★★

7 hours later.

The room is pitch black. The sound of a cigarette lighter is flicking. The lighter finally flicks on. The light brightens her face and the lighter lights the cigarette. The lighter flicks off. It is pitch dark in the room. The only thing that is seen is the light from the cigarette. She turns to the electrical clock and it says10:37 PM. Precious Jewell says,

Damn, it is 10:37. Fuck it, I'm going to the club tonight."
Later on that night at the club. Amura walks through the
club doors. The club is jammed packed with people. The
music of the rap group Whoodini "Funky Beat". Amura
walks through the crowd as they dance on the dance floor.
A female waitress walks by and passes Amura a bottle of
champagne. Amura kisses her on the lips. Amura says,
"Thank you boo." Amura continue to walk through the
crowd to the steps that lead to an office built viewing the
club. In front of the officer door there are two very huge
men standing guard wearing tinted glasses. Amura stops
in front of the men. "If I was to every fuck any men I
would suck all the sperm out of both y'all dicks." The men
smile. Amura walks through the door, there are four
ladies sitting at the round table talking and they are
counting money. Their attention is captured by Amura
presents. Tasha says, "What's going on Ms. Bitch? Let me
get some of that." Tasha grabs a glass off of the table.
Amura walks toward the table and pours the champagne
in the glass. Veryfine says, "We sent for some chicken
from Momma's Fried." Amura replies looking around the
room. "Where's Marquis?" Tawana points to the
bathroom and says, "He is in the bathroom. So, you know
what he is doing." Amura is disgusted, I don't know what
the fuck is his problem. We probably pull off 47 million in

sales, and this motherfucker is no better than a dope head shooting in an abandoned building. Shit the motherfucker done shot up in an abandoned building." The sound of a woman yearning. "Huh, huh, huh, fuck me in my ass harder." Amura says, "Who in the hell is he in there with?" Tasha says, "Some junky bitch! My right hand to Gods face, you would not believe she is a junky." Marquis is in the bathroom with a woman having anal intercourse. Her shirt is unbuttoned. He licks her face. He begins to stroke harder and harder. Marquis I see you like me fucking you in your ass, Michelle. "Fuck me harder." Marquis reaches in the sink to get a syringe filled with heroin. "Stick it in my fucking neck." Marquis sticks the syringe in Michelle's neck.

20 minutes later.

Amura is standing by the door of the bathroom getting ready to knock. Marquis opens the door walking the female out the bathroom. The woman walks out the bathroom barely standing up on her own two feet. Amura stands there watching so is every one else in the room. Michelle says, "Thanks for the get high. Thanks for that little sample you gave me. And of course, fucking me in the ass like that. I'll be seeing you." She walks out of the office. Amura turns to Marquis as he walks out of the bathroom. Amura says, "I guess I don't need to ask what you where doing. Did you put on a condom, you don't need to be giving nobody anything. Marquis smiles. He grabs the champagne bottle out of her hand. Marquis says, "Why would you say that? You know, I'm just doing me. I like it raw like my coke. Marquis walks over to the glass window that over looks the club. He drinks from the bottle. From where Marquis is standing, he sees Precious Jewell walking into the club. Precious Jewell walks into the club. She walks over to the leather-seated booth. Marquis is watching Precious Jewell. Marquis says, "Get the fuck out of here. Look who walk in the motherfuckin door? Precious Jewell. Yo, Amura, come here. Look who's here? Amura walks over to Marquis. Marquis points in the direction Precious Jewell is in. Amura, "Look at her. She reminds me of Sheeka." Tawana walks over to Marquis and Amura. Tawana looks at Amura, "You want me to go get her, right." "Please!" Amura responded. Amura points. "That one right there." Tawana says, "Fly, Tasha. Let's go. Spanish Fly and Tasha leave from the round table and they all walk out of the door. Marquis drinks from the champagne bottle. Amura takes it out of his hand and she drinks. She whispers to Marquis. "Where are we going to dump her body?" They are

42

looking at Veryfine, Amura's girlfriend. The music is loud in the club. People are dancing. Tawana, Spanish Fly, and Tasha walk through the crowd. They walk to the booth where Precious Jewell sits. The women all slide in the booth. Spanish Fly is sitting to the right and Tawana and Tasha to the left of Precious Jewell. Precious Jewell sits her drink on the table. Precious Jewell says, "Now, who are you bitches?" Tasha says, "We some down bitches, down for what ever." Spanish Fly picks up Precious Jewell glass and starts to drink it. "You're going to pay for that." Precious Jewell says. Spanish Fly responds, "It's on the house." Spanish Fly puts the drink down. Spanish Fly slides her knife out of her knife holster on her thigh. She quickly wraps her arms around Precious Jewell neck with the knife to her throat. "Bitch I'll cut your throat." Precious Jewell laughs says, "You are funny, you better cut me." "I'm not going to cut your throat. Somebody wants to meet you." Spanish Fly responds. Spanish Fly puts the knife back in the holster. Tawana says, "Come on. Amura wants to speak with you. Tawana grabs her wrist pulling her. All of the women slide out of the booth. Tawana lets Precious Jewell wrist go. Tawana leads the women though the crowd. They walk to the steps that lead to the office. Inside the office, Amura is standing looking at the crowd dancing. Marquis is sitting at the table burning money. Veryfine is sitting at the table counting money. The women walk through the door of the office. Spanish Fly slams the door. The women stand around. Marquis says, "We got to be careful, we've been getting a lot of fake bills lately." He turns his head. What's the deal?" Precious Jewell says, "What's the deal you sweet talking motherfucker?" Marquis responds with a smile, "Nothing baby girl." Veryfine puts her drink down.

"Who the fuck is this?" Veryfine says loudly. Precious Jewell shouts, "No, who the fuck are you, bitch?" Precious turns her head toward Amura. "Who the fuck are you? You were speaking to Sheeka last night." "Yes I'm Amura, the bitch you love to hate." Precious Jewell responds, " Sheeka told me about you. She told me to stay away from you. I wonder why?" "I'm good people. Some time I'm misunderstood, or some people just need to know the rules of the game. Precious says, O.K., fuck the bullshit, I know y'all got some get high up in here and could you explain that bullshit you just ran by me about my cousin." Marquis gets up from the table walking over to the refrigerator. He opens the refrigerator and there are zip lock bags of coke. He reaches in the refrigerator to get a zip lock bag of coke. Amura says, "So Sheeka is your cousin. Well the only thing I can say is the charge was going to stick on one of us. If I could have got Sheeka out of jail I would have. It is not like I didn't try. It was above my head. Precious Jewell responds, "Shit happens I see. Sheeka got locked up today anyway. So why was I asked to come up here? Marquis walks back over to the table and throughs the zip lock bag of coke on the table. Marquis says, "I call it the party mix." Precious Jewell walks over to the table. She picks up the bag and puts her hand in the bag and takes a big pitch of powder and drops it on the edge of the table. She pushes the coke to the edge of the table. She bends down and snorts the coke. She stands up straight wiping her nose. Her eyes get glossy, and she sniffles. She wipes her nose. "Damn this is some good shit. I bet Sheeka couldn't do it like that. Let me get a cigarette." Amura says, "They're right there on the table." Precious Jewell reaches on the table to get a cigarette from the pack. She gets a lighter from the table and lights the cigarette. She takes a pull and blows the smoke out. "I'm a down bitch or what?" Spanish Fly shouts, "This bitch is bold." Veryfine shouts, "This bitch got a big fucking mouth." Tasha says, "I want to see how this is going down." All the ladies walk over to the table watching Precious Jewell and Veryfine. Amura shouts, "Yo Veryfine, I heard that you been running your fucking mouth about my business." "Baby girl what? Amura says, Don't fuck with me? Yeah bitch, you know what I'm talking about? Veryfine responds with innocence, "What?" She turns to Amura. "Amura what's up baby?"

45

Amura says, "Show me some loyalty. You're going to let this bitch right here take your spot." She turns to Precious Jewell. "I been having an itch and it needs to be scratched." Amura pulls from her waistline a .357 silver Smith and Wesson handgun. She slams it on the table and she spins the gun on the table. "Precious we don't have another day to waist seeing this bitch." The gun stops spinning. The handle stops in front of Precious Jewell. Precious Jewell grabs the gun and shoots. Boom! Veryfine's eye shoots blood out profusely. Blood is all over her face and body. She falls out of the chair. Precious Jewell stands up and walks over to Veryfine and she puts her foot on her chest. Precious Jewell says, "Leave no witnesses." Precious Jewell shoots her in the head. She blows the smoke out of her mouth.

PERFECT PAIR
PUBLICATIONS

CHAPTER 3

THEINVESTIGATION

A black male is riding on a train in Africa. He is looking out of the window-watching people walking in the hot desert sun carrying their possessions. An army regime is marching in the desert with their guns. A sound of a telephone makes him turn his head. Ring, Ring, Ring. The man (Detective Steele) opens his eyes and sunlight is in his face. He turns his head to the phone on the nightstand. The phone is ringing. He reaches over to the nightstand to answer the phone. A voice is heard over the phone. It is captain Marshal "Ay." Dt. Steele replies, "Who's this?" "It's the Captain." "How are you doing sir? What's going on?" "I have some good news, can you come in." "What is it?" "Your suspension is over, they need you on a case. So be here about 11 o'clock." "I'll be there." The detective hangs up the phone and gets out of bed and goes to get in the shower.

★★★

2 hours later at the police prescient.

Police officers are walking in the police station. A police officer walks in with a bag full of marijuana that he found in the cab. He walks to a desk where three officers are sitting down writing reports. The officer says, "Can you believe this shit? Look what I found in the cab." He dumps the marijuana on the table. " It got to be about 30 pounds." Dt. Steele walks into the office. He walks pass the officer, "Don't take any of that home to your kids O.K." The officer shouts, "I don't find that shit funny." Dt. Steele walks to the captain's office. Inside the office, Captain Marshall is sitting at the table looking at some pictures. Dt. Steele walks in the office and closes the door. Dt. Steele says, "Captain how are you doing?" Captain Marshall responds, "I'm fine. Have a seat." Dt. Steele sits down in the chair and Capt. Marshall slides him some pictures. The captain points to the pictures. "These are the photos taken here." The captain points to the pictures from L.A. crime scene. He then he points to the other pictures from N.Y. crime scene. "Those are the photos taken in New York." Capt. Marshall passes Dt. Steele two

PERFECT PAIR PUBLICATIONS....

photos. One from each crime scene, both of the photos has a man and woman burned to death. One of the dead bodies has duck tape around the mouth and one has a syringe in the neck. "So now you're on the case and you have the best of both worlds." Dt. Steele says, "What do you mean?" "You get to work on it here, and in New York. It would be good for you to go back home for a while." Captain Marshall says. Dt Steele shakes his head, "Sir all my family is over here. As far as the ones over there, I don't know. They are dead. And from what I heard, some died of a drug overdose in the 80's. So, when do I leave? And uncle I hate going there. That is where your sister died." Capt. Marshall reaches in his draw and grabs the plane tickets and Dt. Steele's badge and gun. He slides it on the table. Captain Marshall says, "Yeah I know. Tomorrow, 8 o'clock flight. Another thing, the word came down from the mayor's office, he wants this to be over with. This is a joint venture. Neither our mayor nor the mayor in New York wants the Feds to get in on this. The Feds are giving us time to do this our selves. So go there and get this shit solved, bottom line." Dt Steele, says "No problem." Now go home and get some rest. You really got a lot of work to do. Your partner in New York will pick you up from the airport."

★★★

49

30 minutes later a restaurant

Dt Steele walks through the door of the restaurant. He sits down and he takes the pictures out of the envelope. He pulls out a pack of cigarettes and he takes one out. He takes his lighter out his coat pocket and lights the cigarette. A waitress walks over to the table. "Can I take your order?" Dt. Steele responds, "Espresso please." "Right away sir." Dt. Steele picks the pictures up from the table and blows the smoke at the pictures. He stares at the pictures of a burned body and imagines a woman on fire.

★★★

5 hours later at J.F.K. Airport in New York City

People are walking in an out of the airport terminal with their luggage. Dt. Steele walks through the door to go outside the terminal. He has the 70's look, big glasses and ¾ leather jacket. A man is standing outside with cardboard with Dt. Steele's name. It is a hip white detective (Dt.) Jadean . Dt. Jadean shouts, "Where the fuck is he? He is an hour late." Dt Steele turns in Dt. Jadean direction and sees him standing there with the cardboard box with Dt. Steele name on it. He shouts, "Yo, I'm Dt. Steele." Dt. Steele walks over there to him. "I'm Dt. Jadean, but you can call me Jay." They give one another a handshake. "Well, I'll be your partner on the case." Dt. Steele pulls out a cigarette from his coat pocket. "You got a light." Dt. Jadean responds, "Yeah." Dt. Jadean pulls out the lighter and flicks it on. Dt. Steele lights his cigarette. He inhales the smoke and blows it out. Dt. Steele says, "Thanks, by the way, how old are you." "28, and you." "41" Dt Steele says with a smile. Dt. Jadean says, "I see you don't have any bags." "I carry light. I'll buy some clothing while I'm here. Only thing I got is, these files in my hand and my gun. So where is the ride?" Dt. Jadean responds, "Right here." He points to the car. It is a black Chevy Utility Van. They both get into the jeep. Dt. Jadean is on the driver's side and Dt. Steele on the passenger side. Dt. Jadean starts the SUV and drives off out of the airport to the expressway. Dt. Steele pulls out a photo from the envelope. Dt. Steele says, "Damn I want to know what the fuck is the motive behind this shit." He sighs. He puts the photo back inside. "So what do you carry?" Dt. Steele pulls out a Glock .40. Dt. Steele says, "All the time." Dt. Jadean responds, "Oh, that's real pretty but this." Dt. Jadean moves his jacket back. He has a Tec.22 assault rifle in a holster strapped to his chest. "This is just my back-up gun." They laugh. "So how long you've been on the force?" Dt. Steele responds, "18 years and you." Dt. Jadean says, "My father was a cop back in the 70's, he got gunned down when I was 4 years old. So

I'm just really keeping his spirit alive. You know?" "Yeah, I know exactly what you talking about, "Where are you from?" Dt. Steele responds, "From Brooklyn. I stayed to about 11 years old. I really don't have any close contact with any of my family that's here. All of my family is in L.A." Dt. Jadean's cellular phone rings. He takes the phone out of his jacket pocket and put it to his ear. "Hello!" A female's voice is heard over the phone "You got our guy?" "Yeah, we are on the Grand Central Expressway." "Good, cause we got another murder." "Male or female." "Female white. She is uptown on 130th street and 5th Ave, the motel on the corner. Her throat was slashed. They found a syringe in her arm. And Jadean, go in your glove compartment and get the vicks, because it really stinks inside the apartment." "All right Jackie, we're there. Bye." He puts the phone back in his jacket pocket. Dt. Steele says, "What's up?" Dt. Jadean responds, "We got another one, it's a woman." "That's where we at." "With out a doubt." Dt. Steele and Dt. Jadean pull off at the next exit.

★★★

20 minutes later the are at the murder scene. There are cop cars parked in front of a building. Dt. Jadean and Dt. Steele pulls up and double-park the car next to a cop car. Dt. Jadean opens the glove compartment to get a small jar of vicks. "We are going to need this. Jackie said it really stinks up there. Damn I didn't even ask her what floor." They both get out of the van walking to the entrance of the building. It is a ran down looking motel. The owner of the building is standing at the doorway. The owner of the building is a short fat white guy with glasses smoking a cigar. Dt. Jadean says, "Was there an officer posted here?" The Owner of building says, "What, who are you?" Dt. Jadean says, "N.Y.P.D." Owner responds, "Just to let you know I own this castle and as for the New York finest, he just ran to the bathroom. He told me to stand post. He said he had to take a shit. An officer is on the way down right now. You said NYPD. That's that shit. That's that disease that kills black men." Dt. Jadean stares at Dt. Steele and turns back to the owner. A police officer is walking down the stairs. An officer is walking toward them through the lobby of the building. "How about I strap my badge to this boot and stomp you with it?" The police officer walks up. Dt. Jadean turns to the officer. "Richardson, run a fucking warrant check on this bastard." Officer Richardson responds, "Yes sir." "That's not fair" he says loudly. Dt. Jadean gets up close to Jadean barks, "I don't give a fuck!" "I could sue if you lay a hand on me." Dt. Jadean gets closer to the owner's face. "Listen, I'm white and aggravated. I will fuck you up and drag you in the alley. And I'm a cop, so ask me if I care if you sue. The million that you'll get from the city will go to your doctor fees." The owner responds quickly, "7J, at the end, on your right." Dt. Jadean goes in his pocket and takes out a dime. He tosses it at the owner. Dt. Jadean and Dt. Steele walk in the building through the doors to the elevator. A cop gets off the elevator walking past Dt. Jadean and Dt. Steele. Officer Huggins, "How are you doing? I think Brian shitted on himself." They get on the elevator and Dt. Steele presses the button 7. The elevator doors closes. Dt. Steele shakes his head. "Damn, I see that another mother will be at the funeral crying." Dt. Jadean shakes his head taking a deep breath. They reached the 7th floor. A police officer is standing guard on the floor. The two detectives exit the elevator. Officer Porter, "It is about time you got here. I heard from the Captain that you would be investigating the murder. And this must be your partner from L.A. The officer and Dt. Steele shake hands. Dt. Steele says, "How are you doing?" 'Tired of wearing these hard as shoes. The apartment is 7J." The officer points. "Right down the hall." The detectives walk down the hallway to the apartment. There is an officer standing guard at apartment 7J. Insents are being burned for the stench in the air. They walk into the apartment. Dt.

Jadean pulls out the small jar of vicks from his jacket. He opens the jar and dips his finger in the petroleum and puts a little under his nose. He passes it to Dt. Steele and he does the same thing. Dt. Jadean puts the vicks back in his jacket pocket. There are police officers investigating the crime scene. Flashes of light from the camera light the room. They walk up to one of the investigating detectives'. Dt. Jadean taps him on the shoulder. The detective turns around. He has an evidence bag in his hand. Dt. Lewis says, " How are you doing Jadean? This woman that was killed, she was brought in for questioning last week about a murder. It was drug related. A new high grain of heroin has hit the street and 10 people have died. Word on the street, her brother was selling the shit. Unfortunately, her brother was one of the 10 people that died from shooting that shit. A needle was found in her arm. We didn't touch anything. We were waiting for you. Also, we went to all the apartments on the floor and told everyone that they had to leave until we finish investigating. Come this way, the body is in here." They all walk to the room where the dead body is. Dt. Jadean says, "Fine." This is my partner from L.A. Dt. Steele." Dt. Steele and the detective shake hands. Anything that is found let me know. And anything I know, my partner here should know." Dt. Lewis says, "No problem." Investigating officers are in the room taking pictures of the room, checking the room for evidence, and examining the dead body. There is a white female tied to a chair sitting up with here throat slashed. The woman is naked with high heel shoes on. The blood on her body is dried up. Her body is pail and rigormortis has stiffened her body. A syringe is sticking in her right arm. Dt. Jadean, Dt. Lewis, Dt. Steele walk into the room. Dt. Jadean says, "How did the report come to notice?" Dt. Lewis responds, "An old lady from next door called in and said she smelled something funny. And she said that the female would usually bring her the paper every morning. Dt. Steele asked, "Did any one on the floor see or hear anything?" He shakes his head. I can't believe it. There was a murder just like this in L.A. Murdered and left for dead, just like that." He points to the woman. Dt. Lewis says, "We did ask everyone on the floor and they said they didn't see or hear anything, but they did say that this apartment always had females running in and out of here at night." Dt. Steele walks closer to the dead body and looks the lady up and down. "Were pictures taken for this already?" The photographer turns around and respond. "Yes. I took five different shots from all different angles. The photographer takes another shot of the bed. "And I think that is about it sir. I will have these photos developed as soon as I get back to the station. Dt. Jadean walks over to the body and says, "Who in the hell could have done this?" He shakes his head turning to look at Dt. Steele. "Hey, they did send you here for this type of shit." Dt. Steele stares at the dead body and says, "A murder in Compton was carried out just like this. Very little evidence left behind, but nothing that gave us a lead." Dt. Jadean replies, "They must do their shit right. It must be a small group, maybe three or four, or maybe a copycat murderer. We've got murders here, you got murders there, so either the murderer has some buddies or he's one busy motherfucker. Dt. Steele says, "Who is to say it's a male? Or I must not have gotten much sleep coming from L.A. here." A detective walks in with the pad and pen in his hand. Dt. Jadean turns to look at the detective. "Aye, did you find anything yet, prints, hair strains?" Dt. Fields responds, " It's bagged already. The only strains we found so far were in the bathroom. We found hairbrushes, washrags and towels, and we took toothbrushes also. We also found a used condom. Something will show up. We already dust for fingerprints, it's all been sent to central. They have a new database operation system down there. As for the hair samples and the bodily fluids, it will take a week or so for the DNA." Dt. Jadean says, "Thanks, I'm going down to the Medical Examiner's Office." Dt. Jadean and Dt. Steele walk out off the apartment to the elevator. Dt. Jadean and Dt. Steele exits through the door. Dt. Jadean turns to Dt. Steele while walking. Dt. Steele says,

"We need to get downtown quick." Dt. Jadean responds, " Just what I was thinking. Let's jump on this shit right away." They walk to the double-parked utility van. They both get in, Dt. Steele on the passenger side and Dt. Jadean on the drivers side. They drive off in the van.

20 minutes later.

Dt. Jadean and Dt. Steele both walk through the door of the coroner's office. There are four dead bodies lying on the steel table beds. The coroner is looking at the paper with results from a test. The two detective walk over to the coroner. Dt Jadean says, "What's the deal?" The Coroner responds, "I rushed the fingerprints. All the fingerprints found in that apartment uptown matched all of the dead bodies in here. All of them tested positive for heroin and Hepatitis C. Also I found out that there was a different blood type from all of them next to the puncture wounds in their arms. It's blood type A. So they were sharing the same needle with the same person. Two white males had their throats slashed. One black male and one black female, both of them shot in the head, doused with gasoline, then set on fire in an alley. So you might be dealing with a serial killer. So these are the people that probably could help you. The only thing is they can't talk to you because they are dead. A dead man tells no tales. I'm waiting for the body from uptown to get here. I hear that this is your case. I wish you luck." Dt. Steele says, "What made you check the fingerprints?" Coroner replies, "I use to be a detective. It's a giveaway." Dt. Jadean says, "Damn, that eliminates all of our leads. Dt. Fields walks through the door. Dt. Fields says to the coroner, "Jim, I put the evidence in the other room with Mary. He turns to Dt. Jadean. "Jadean, an old lady that was on vacation just returned to the building who lives on the floor said that there were always women walking into that apartment. But, she is blind in one eye and partially in the other. Dt. Jadean, says, "Thanks for nothing Ted." Dt. Fields responds, "You're welcome. And by the way, the captain is here and he wants to see you and your partner." Dt Steele says, "Does that building have cameras?" "No. Not at all. It's a fucking motel." The Captain walks through the door. Captain Alerte says, "What's the deal Jadean?" "Sir we are on it. And sir, here is my partner from L.A." The Captain and Dt. Steele stare at one another. Dt. Steele puts his hand out to greet the Captain. Dt. Steele speaks to the captain, "Hello sir, my name is Omar Steele." They shake hands. So what is the deal? You know what, fuck the deal, just find out who is behind this shit? Jadean I put you on the case because I know you get shit done right and exact. So I'm expecting you to be at your best. He turns to Dt. Steele. I talked to your Captain and he said that you are his best man on homicides in Compton. "And sir, I know that these are not drive by shootings." "That's just the answer I wanted to here. O.K. fellas I want to go on vacation and I while I'm on vacation I want to fuck my wife real good."

8 Months Later At The Police Station

Pictures of murder victims are hung on the wall. A burned female and male body, a female and male with a syringe in their arm and a bullet wound to their head, a female tied to a the chair with a syringe in her arm, and two men with their throats slashed. The Captain is standing looking at the photos. Dt. Jadean and Dt. Steele are sitting in the chairs looking at the Captain. The Captain is not aware that Dt. Jadean is nodding off to sleep because he has on these big 1970 dark shade glasses on. The Captain turns to address the both of them. Capt. Alerte shouts, "What the fuck seems to be the problem? I remember 8 months ago I ask y'all to get this shit done. You're not eating your fucking wheates." The captain focuses his attention to Jadean. "Get your ass up Jadean." Dt. Jadean is startled by the Captains voice and now he is wide-awake. *"You see this shit that is hanging on my wall. Do something about it. Prevent shit like this from happening. You are the youngest, but indeed the best detective on the squad, probably in the whole fucking city and you and your buddy from L.A. hasn't found shit. It's been 9 murders since you two been on the case. I want to go on vacation, you heard me. The both of you get the fuck out of here and find out who the fuck is behind this shit, because if it's not done soon, the FEDS will be taking over. And if they take over, they will be looking through a lot of the caseloads. I want to go on vacation. My doctor just gave me some Viagra. I want to fuck my wife real good while we are on vacation. I think the bitch is fucking my brother. But that's another story." He sighs. "On a serious note, go out there fellas and get some bad guys. And guys, find out what this shit is about." The Captain points to the pictures. Dt. Jadean and Dt. Steele both stand up and say, "Yes sir."*

Across Town At The Club

Amura, Spanish Fly, Tasha, Tawana, and Precious Jewell are sitting at a round table with a black female who has AIDS. Visually the female is sickened. She has black spots all over her face. They are looking at the big flat screen T.V. They are watching the news. The new reporter says, "In other news, FBI confirmed that the body washed up

61

on Coney Island beach was indeed drug trafficker Lorenzo Andrews. It's reported that he had ties to the Black Guerrilla Family and militant regimes in Africa. FBI sources say that he trafficked more than 700 million dollars of heroin into the country over the past 16 years." Amura turns the T.V. off with the remote control. Amura says, "This is what needs to be done, I'll give you $100,000 if you kill someone for me. I can't do it because of the treaty, but you can do it for me. See he fucked up. 10 million dollars in off shore accounts turned up missing and we know that he did it. And are you taking your medication. The medication that they have now is better then what they had years ago." Female with AIDS responds, "My T-Cells are down and the medication is not working. I don't have HIV I have AIDS. If anything on this planet that needs to be killed is AIDS. This bastard from Africa you want me to kill, I've read somewhere that his father was there when HIV was put in some vaccines in the 60's. You know what, I'll strap a bomb on my chest, and blow that motherfucker up. I'm going to die any away, before I go, I know y'all got some free base in here." Spanish Fly says, "Precious, go in the fridge and get the hard white." Precious Jewell gets up from the table and walks over to the refrigerator. She opens the door. There are zip lock bags of heroin, cocaine, and crack cocaine.

She reaches for the block of crack cocaine. Precious Jewell walks back over to the table and tosses the bag on the table. The female with AIDS pulls out a crack pipe from her coat pocket and lays it on the table. Female with AIDS says, "Any one of you got a fucking razor blade." Spanish Fly takes her knife from her holster and slides it across the table. The female grabs the knife and reaches for the bag. She pulls out a big piece of crack cocaine out of the bag and places it on the table. She takes the knife and slices a piece to put in her pipe. She takes the piece and sticks it in her pipe. She lights the crack pipe and begins to suck the smoke and exhales the smoke. I heard somewhere that the biggest trick that the devil did was made the people on the planet believe that he didn't existed. That is what the AIDS virus does to the human body. Makes the body believe that it doesn't existed after the virus replicates itself to look normal. A vaccine must be created to identify the virus when it is the human body. The same effect the polio vaccine did with the polio virus. The people need to know that this is the only way to stop this. She inhales and exhales the smoke from the crack pipe. "So where is this motherfucker? Amura, promise me you give that money to my daughter, she just had a baby and some form of AIDS research. Shit 64% of Black American woman tested are positive for this shit. Maybe if I was sucking some pussy like you, then I would not have this problem. Fucking with those jive talking ass niggas. And Amura, your brother is going to end up like me. He needs to be careful with whom he's shooting with. I saw him at the hole in the wall shooting up with someone who I heard got AIDS. I don't know if he shared the needle, but he needs to be careful." Amura responds, "I'll let him know. And I promise your daughter will get the money." The female lights the crack pipe again. She inhales then exhales the crack smoke. Female with AIDS "So where is he?"

3 Hours Later In Front Of The African Embassy

An African male is standing in front of the embassy flagging for a cab. The street is crowded with cars caught in a traffic jam. It is very noisy from the sound of car horns. The people in the cars are cursing about the traffic jam. Dt. Jadean and Dt. Steele are caught in the traffic jam. Dt. Steele and Dt. Jadean are sitting in the car. Dt Jadean is cursing about the traffic jam. Dt. Steele's cellular phone rings. Dt. Jadean says, "What the fuck is going on up there." Dt. Steele answers his cellular phone. "Hello." Dt. Jadean does not pay any attention to Dt. Steele phone call. He takes notice to a female walking

64

across the street. It is the female with AIDS walking across the street. Dt. Jadean says, "Ain't this a motherfucker! I wish this vehicle could move like that woman right now." Dt. Steele has his cellular phone in his ear. He responds to the person he is speaking to on the phone. "I see everything is everything." He hangs up the phone and puts it in his pocket. "The lady speeds up her step walking toward the African man. She walks up to him and hugs him firmly. The African man speaks. "Who the hell are you? Get off of me." The African male struggles to get her off. The female and the male blow up into pieces. Their body parts are all over the pavement. People in the street are frantic. Women are screaming. Smoke fills the air from the remaining body parts that are left there on the pavement. Dt. Jadean and Dt. Steele gets out of the utility vehicle with their police badges out. Dt. Jadean and Dt. Steele runs over to the pavement. They cannot believe what they have just seen. They are looking at the body parts. Dt. Jadean yells, "What the fuck was that shit all about? This is something that you see in the movies. Damn let me call this in Dt. Jadean walks back to the utility van. Across the street, Precious Jewell and Amura are sitting in a car across the street from the explosion. The car windows are tinted. They are looking at Dt. Steele. Precious Jewell says, "Let's get the fuck out of here. That cop is looking right at us." Precious Jewell slumps down in the car seat. The traffic starts to move quickly, it is no longing a traffic jam. Amura rolls down the window and pulls off into the traffic. Amura is looking at Dt. Steele smiling and Dt. Steele is looking at her pulling off into the traffic.

CHAPTER 4
THE ENFORCERS

Amura, Spanish Fly, Precious Jewell, Tawana, and Tasha are at a round table sitting with four African men. The four African men have on sunglasses smoking cigarettes. The ladies have two very big body guards standing behind them. Spanish Fly stands up out of the chair. Spanish Fly says "You are paid to move that shit across your country. We don't give a fuck how you do it, we want the motherfucker done. Bottom line! One of the African Males say, "You know what, don't talk to me like that. I'm not a cotton picker. I'm not from this country. I'm African. My ancestors sold yours like fucking cattle." Amura replies, "Listen, fuck all the bullshit." All of the women draw out their guns pointing at the African men. Spanish Fly walks quickly over to the African male that was talking and put the gun to his head. "Don't any of you reach for your guns?" Amura stands with her gun drawn. "You are going to get those people in the village that got AIDS to carry the heroin here to the states. They need medical care. They are not going to get searched when going through customs. They got United Nation's visa's to get into the United States. If they allowed that sand nigga Sadaam Hussein to sneak oil out of his country with the oil for food program, then we are not going to have a problem. Ours is high grain heroin for AIDS medication mother fucker. When your people make it to the final destination, then the exchange for the best fucking AIDS medication on the market will be given to them." Spanish Fly cocks the hammer back on her nickel platted .357. Spanish Fly snatches the Africa male's sunglasses off his face. "Tell Mr. Imean its money to be made and we are giving up more than enough. The people who we supply are down to do whatever, any of your countrymen come here will be killed if we have this conversation again. Tell that motherfucker over there, he better do what he's told. Our money put his ass in power. You heard!" The man with the gun to his head, nodes his head agreeing.

2 days later in Africa
The sun is setting over the village. Inside a large hut there are ten African women sitting on the floor at the table.

LORENZO ANDREWS

The table is filled with powder (heroin) scattered all around. Electrical scales, spoons, and latex balloons filled with heroin are also on the table. The women at the table are sitting there as if they are standing attention for a drill sergeant in the army, but they are looking at Marquis and an African man with a gun in his hand. Marquis is standing next to the window on the phone. Marquis is speaking to Amura, "Everything is everything. I'm getting ready to send it now. The plane is scheduled to land in Amsterdam at 1:30. After we leave Amsterdam, we should be in the states by 11:30. A voice is heard on the phone. It is Amura. "Are you taking care of yourself? Don't be fucking with that shit. Take care of business. Marquis replies, "What's up with Precious?" A click is heard. Amura hangs up the phone. Marquis hangs the phone up by closing it. He looks at the African man. "Yo let's go. I got to get back to New York. I have a plane to catch." The African man speaks his native language. The women put an oil base liquid on the balloons. They pick the balloons off of the table and swallow them. If that shit bust in their stomachs, they are some dead motherfuckers. Their bodies will be on the floor like a fish out of water."

2 days later back in New York City

Amura, Tasha, Precious Jewell, Spanish Fly, and Tawana are sitting at the round table smoking and drinking champagne. There are stacks of money on the table. There is a small pile of cocaine and an ace of spade card is on the table, not to far in front of Amura and their guns are on the table. Spanish Fly says, "We had to make a lot of money at the bar tonight." Amura shouts, "What's up? Let's get high before we go. "She looks at every body. "Call me a hypocrite." Spanish Fly says, "Hypocrite. Shit I'm going home. I'm tired." Amura reaches for a card that is on the table and slips the card under the cocaine. She sniffs the powder off the card. Her eyes get glossy. She says, "Damn this is some good shit." The ladies get up from the table. Tawana, Spanish Fly, and Tasha grab their jackets off the chairs they were sitting in and their guns off of the table. Tawana says, "I see y'all later on today." Tasha says, "Let's go to the diner." "It's find with me." Tawana replied. Tawana, Spanish Fly, and Tasha leave out of the office slamming the door. Precious Jewell says, "You're not going to offer me none. Amura laughs as she stares at Precious Jewell." "What the fuck you're thinking about?" "What are you looking at, how hard my nipples are right? Every time I see coke, that shit get my nipples hard." Amura says, "Why don't you come sit here on my lap and let me sniff some of this off of your nipples?"

AN EMOTIONAL HOMICIDE

Precious Jewell walks slowly toward Amura licking her lips. She stands in front of Amura. Precious Jewell says, "Why don't you lick it out of my ass hole?" "I see that you are a nasty girl. You know I can be there emotionally for you because I know how a woman is supposed to be loved. I can be there for you physically because I know how a pussy is supposed to be sucked. Because I'm a woman." Precious Jewell lifts up her skirt. She has on thong underwear. She bends over on the table with her ass in Amura's face. Amura slaps her on the ass. Precious Jewell turns around and sits on Amura's lap. Precious Jewell takes off her blouse and her breast is showing. Amura reaches for the ace of spade card and swipes some coke on the card and puts it on Precious Jewell's breast. She then puts the card to Precious Jewell's nose. Precious Jewell sniffs the rest of the coke on the card. She takes the card out of Amura's hand and licks the card. She flings the card on the floor. Amura sniffs the coke off Precious Jewell's breast then she starts to suck her nipples. Marquis walks in the door quietly smoking a cigarette. He sees Precious Jewell and Amura getting it on. Marquis whispers, "Ain't this a motherfucker?" Precious Jewell is staring at Marquis, biting her lip. She has this evil looking smirk on her face.

★★★

71

The Next Day

At a beauty salon a beautician is washing another female's hair. A woman in sunglasses dressed in a trench coat walks in the beauty salon. It is Spanish Fly. Spanish Fly pulls out a sawed off double barrel shotgun from her trench coat. She shoots the beautician in the stomach. The beautician falls on the floor. She then shoots the woman who is getting her hair washed in the head. The woman head is blown off. Her brains is all over place. An our later another murder is committed, Tawana is sitting in the driver's seat and Tasha sitting in the passenger seat. They are driving down the street in a tinted car. They stop right next to a Cadillac. It is a black man with sunglasses sitting in the car reading a newspaper. Tasha rolls the window down. She sticks a .357 revolver out of the window and shoots the man in the head. Boom! Tawana and Tasha speeds off in the car. The man's blood is all over the dashboard and the passenger's seat. The man's body is slump over in the driver's seat. Later on that night. Amura and Precious Jewell are at a club. There are people in the bathroom getting high and having sex while listening to the music. The music being played is Method Man's "Bring The Pain". Precious Jewell and Amura are sniffing coke of a card with a white male standing next to the toilet with the door close. The white male say, "This is some good shit Amura. How much is this shit a gram?" Amura responds, "Fuck the bullshit! Where is my money?" "I told you that I dump the shit in the toilet because the police bust in the door." Amura barks back, "I don't give a fuck." The white male gets face to face with Amura. "What the fuck you are going to do?" He turns to Precious Jewell. "Who the fuck are you?" The white males has his eyes on Precious Jewell and Amura pulls out an ice picks and stabs him in the throat 4 times. Blood flows out of his throat. He tries to talk but cannot be heard. The white male grabs his throat and falls on the floor bleeding to death. Amura and Precious walk out and closes the door. People are having sex and using drugs. Amura and Precious Jewell walk out of the bathroom. A couple of hours pass and the police are questioning the people who were in the bathroom. All off the people are stoned from getting high. Dt. Steele and Dt. Jadean walk into the club. They walk through the crowd of police into the bathroom. Dt. Jadean and Dt. Steele walks into the bathroom. The police are taken pictures of the white male's dead body. The body lies in a pool of blood do to the stabbing from Amura. Flashes of light from the camera light the bathroom. Dt. Jadean and Dt. Steele walk to the investigating officer who is looking at the dead body. Dt. Steele says, "How in the hell they are going to get anything out of these fucking losers? All of them are high.

So there testimony would be useless anyway." Dt. Jadean responds, "Let's see what we can fine." Dt Brown shouts, "Detective over here." Dt. Jadean and Dt. Steele look in the direction of the officer and they walk over to where the dead body is. The dead body is lying there in an odd position. The white male eyes are open. Cocaine powder is under his nose. Dt. Jadean says, "Look here, we've been investigating this asshole. He does have a rap sheet. A bust just went down three months ago. His ass was in the bathroom dumping the drugs in the toilet. We only charged him with criminal mischief. We tried to get the judge to keep him in the system." Dt .Brown shakes his head and says, "A body was found chopped in the garbage can. That person we found was going to snitch him out." He points to the dead body. "Damn, it's like someone is covering their tracks. Every step." Dt. Steele says, "That's why we were brought to investigate this." Dt. Steele bends down to look at the dead male on the floor. "How long has he been here?" "The report came in about 3 hours ago. 1:04AM." "Were there any witnesses." Dt. Brown responds, "No one saw anything. But some say they seen Jesus and E.T. And that person had a fresh open wound from shooting smack. Dt., everyone in this place was getting high. The Capt. said to still take everyone down and book them all." Dt. Jadean says, "That's going to be a waste of time." Dt. Jadean turns and he sees syringes, powder (heroin and coke), crack pipes and used condoms. Other than all of this shit lying around here, was there any evidence, ID, something that can give us a lead." Dt. Brown says, "We found a card in his back pocket." Officer Brown calls for the cop that has the evidence in the plastic zip lock. Dt. Steele reaches for the bag. "This is it. Nothing else." Dt. Steele is looking at the bag. There is a card inside the zip lock that says, "The Ballroom". Dt. Jadean says, "Oh yeah, that's the club where they have jazz and hip-hop music. But I notice there is always a lot of females there. Dt Steele says, "Well I do like females. I'll jump on this lead.

PERFECT PAIR
PUBLICATIONS

CHAPTER 5
THE LEAD

People are on the dance floor and sitting down listing to a jazz band play music. The room is slightly filled with smoke from the cigarettes and cigars. The people that are sitting down are also drinking champagne. Amura and Precious Jewell are sitting in the back of the club smoking and drinking. Dt. Steele walks through the door of the club. Precious Jewell eyes are on Dt. Steele. Dt. Steele walks over to the bar to order a drink. Other people are sitting at the bar also. Dt. Steele says, "Let me get a shot of Hennessey." A female bartender is washing glasses. The Bartender replies, "Don't you see me doing something?" "And I only see you back there by yourself." "So you are going to wait for your order, you heard me." Dt. Steele answers back, "Can I speak to a manager about getting help or I'm going to pull my gun out, and put it on the table and I'm going to ask you again. Dt. Steele takes his gun out of the holster strapped to his chest. He puts the gun on the bar table. The bartender stops washing the dishes. She dries her hands. The Bartender utters, "What do you want to drink?" Precious Jewell is looking at Dt. Steele from across the room. Amura is enjoying the music not paying any attention to Dt. Steele. She lights a cigarette and inhales very deeply. She blows the smoke out of her nose. Precious Jewell says, "Get the fuck out of here." Precious Jewell can't believe that Dt. Steele is in the club. She gets a flashback to when her and Amura was sitting in the car when Dt. Steele was looking right at them after the bomb explosion. She comes back out of her day dream. "That is the cop who was in front of the hotel when that bitch blew-up the African dude." "Precious Jewell taps Amura on the shoulder and points in the direction where Dt. Steele is sitting." Amura says, "Get the fuck out of here." Amura stares in the direction of Dt. Steele. He receives his drink and swallows the Hennessey from the shot glass and turns in the direction to Amura and Precious Jewell. Precious Jewell shocked that Dt. Steele is looking in at her, "That motherfucker is looking right over here." Amura says, "Go see what he wants. Basically, go see why that motherfucker is in my club." Precious Jewell slides from the booth. "Boo, come give me a kiss." Precious Jewell bends over and licks Amura tongue with a lot of spit. Precious Jewell walks through the crowd toward Dt. Steele. Precious Jewell sits next to Dt. Steele. She orders her drink." Let me get a Thug Passion, red." Precious Jewell turns to Dt. Steele. Dt. Steele says, "Thug Passion, um, Thug Passion. Do you really have a thug in you?" Precious Jewell gives Dt. Steele a hard stare and licks her lips. Precious Jewell says, I'm more of a lover than a fighter." "Where are you from?" Precious Jewell response "I'm not from here." Dt. Steele says, "You have a suspicious look." "What the hell is a suspicious look, is this your first time here?" "Yeah!" Dt. Steele stares at her body. From her pretty toes back up to her pretty face. As he looks back up to her face, Precious Jewell blows smoke in his face. "I love a sassy woman." I love an independent black man, especially a man who is not living in his mother's basement. Do you live in your mother's basement? "He respond quickly, "No, I don't live in my mother's basement. She's dead." "I'm sorry to hear that. So what do you do?" She puts the cigarette on the ashtray that is on the bar table. "I'm a cop." Precious Jewell stares at his watch. Precious Jewell says, "Cops wear expensive watches." Dt. Steele looks at his Rolex watch it is filled with diamonds. "Actually it's a birthday present." "So you are a fucking cop." "No, I'm a detective, still a fucking cop." "So why are you here?" Dt .Steele answers,

"For the same reason you are here, having a drink." "So what are you doing after you have your drink?" She blows smoke from the cigarette in his face. "Do you mind, please don't blow smoke in my face." He flags the smoke out of his face. "I'm going to have another drink." Precious Jewell ask, "After you have that drink." Dt. Steele drinks from the shot glass and slams it down. "Bartender hit me one more time." "How many of those can you take?" "Let's go to my place and see." Precious Jewell replies, "Go to a cop's house, you must be crazy!" "It isn't nothing wrong with coming with me, not at least you did a crime. Besides I'm from L.A., you should know how we get down. You know about my man Mark Fuhrman." "Actually I'll pass on that one." There is silence between the two. He finishes his drink. Precious Jewell questioned him "So where are we headed? They both move toward one another, looking into each other's eyes.

1 hour later

They are in a hotel room. The bright light from the bathroom lights part of the room. The room is lit with candles. There is a beam of light that is spotted directly on the bed where Precious Jewell and Dt. Steele is having sex. The moans and yearning of Precious Jewell gets louder and louder. Dt. Steele has Precious Jewell in a

Doggy Style position. Dt. Steele flips her over and grabs her legs stretching them back. Precious Jewell is biting her lip. Precious Jewell says, "Please put it back in my ass." Dt. Steele says, "You like it like that." Precious Jewell shouts. "Yes, please." Dt. Steele puts it back in her asshole and Precious Jewell moans. Dt. Steele is stroking her harder and harder. "I'm about to cum. Please do it harder", Precious Jewell shouts. Both of them are sweating. Precious Jewell and Dt. Steele both release their orgasms. They both look at one another. Making eye-to-eye contact. Sweat drips from their faces. "Damn that was good. I never got fucked in my ass." Dt. Steele kisses her on the neck. "It's all natural baby." "So that means that you can do it again, old man. You sure you don't need Viagra." Dt. Steele gets off of her and smiles. "I'm going to take a shower." Dt. Steele walks into the bathroom naked. He turns on the shower. Precious Jewell sits up on the bed. She looks on the nightstand on her side of the bed, there is a pack of cigarettes and a lighter. She turns on the lamb light and she reaches for the light and takes a cigarette out of the pack. She lights her cigarette and takes a long pull from the cigarette and blows it out. Dt. Steele is in the shower. The steam from the shower fills the bathroom. He takes of his condom and drops it in the toilet. Dt. Steele shouts, "Are you going to get in here with me?" She shouts, "Yeah boo." They shout back and forth. "I need you to come wash my back." Let me finish smoking my cigarette. Dt. Steele turns on the shower radio. The jazz music plays. Precious Jewell lies back on the bed smoking the cigarette. Her naked body is shining from the sweat from her body. The blanket is partially on her. She looks around the room. She looks at the candles that are around the room. She turns her head to the other stand and she notices that Dt. Steele's gun and a folder is sitting on the nightstand next to the lamp. She rolls over and picked up his gun. "Damn, this motherfucker is big." She reads the side of the gun. Glock 40. She puts the gun back on the table. She picks up the folder and opens it. There is picture of a woman (Veryfine) Precious Jewell shot in the face. She moves the picture and there is another picture of a woman's head blown off at the beauty salon. Precious Jewell is shocked. Precious Jewell whispers, "Get the fuck out of here." Dt. Steele walks up from behind her and grabs her hand. He scares the shit out of her. "Hey that is police business. I'm investigating some murders. The same murders that are happening here are happening in LA. That's why I'm here. Dt. Steele reaches for the pictures and Precious Jewell passes it to him. He puts the pictures back in the folder and then he puts it on the nightstand. "What is so fucked up about this is we don't have any leads, besides that's police business. I could arrest you for that." Precious Jewell says, "Do you have your handcuffs? I want you to do that thing you just did before. I love the smell of sex in the air. My pussy juices still got my asshole wet. Precious Jewell lies back on the bed smiling licking her lips pitching her nipples. Dt. Steele climbs on top of her.

★★★

Early that morning

Precious Jewell lays in the bed filled with red bud roses. Dt. Steele walks out of the bathroom drying his hands. He has already put on his clothing and has his coat on. He walks to the window to let a little sunlight in. There is cart with a silver platted tray with breakfast in it. Dt. Steele roles the cart over to the bed. He walks over to the nightstand and picks up his gun and puts it inside his holster that is strapped to his chest. Dt. Steele says, "Wake up baby, I ordered some breakfast." He takes the lid off of the tray. There are pancakes, eggs, bacon and a glass of orange juice on the top of the tray. He puts the lid on the bottom of the cart. He walks over to the bed to wake Precious Jewell. He shakes her. "Come on baby girl get up." Precious Jewell moans as she wakes up. She opens her eyes and sees that the whole entire bed is filled with red rose buds. Precious Jewell says, "Oh baby this is the sweetest thing some one has ever done for me." She sits up and grabs a hand full of rose buds from the bed. She smells the rose buds. "They smell so good." "You like it, you know I never met any one like you. Shit I had plenty of one-night stands, but I never brought them breakfast and never filled the bed with rose buds. So when I'm I going to see you again. You must have love fucking me in my ass. But then again, I never had a man fuck me in my ass. When I'm I going to see you again?" "I got to get back to work on those murders. I have to go meet my partner and speak to his captain. Also I must send a report back to L.A. on my progress. Here take my card, my number is on it. Dt. Steele reaches for the card out of his coat pocket and passes it to Precious Jewell. "Give me a call. I'm going to see you tonight." Precious Jewell response, "If I'm not busy, I'll call you." "Dt. Steele and Precious Jewell at the same time move toward one another and kiss. Later on that day in the afternoon. It is raining. Precious Jewell is looking out the window of a utility van as the raindrops run down the window. Tawana, Amura, Tasha, and Spanish Fly are also sitting inside a utility van across from the hotel. It is the same hotel that Dt. Jadean and Dt. Steele went to when investigating a murder, when Dt. Steele first arrived. All of the females are dressed in long trench coats. Tawana is sitting in the drivers' seat smoking a cigarette pulling the top of her gun and releasing it to snap back in place. Spanish Fly is looking at her knife. Tasha and Amura are both smoking a joint. Precious Jewell just looks out of the window. Tawana says, "When I was younger, I use to be scared of guns." Tasha asks, "So what happened?" Everyone in the car starts to pay attention to the conversation. "I met this guy, his name was Mike. He was a drug dealer. He taught me how to use a gun. Just in case someone ever rolled on us in the street. Amura counters, " I remember Mike, he was all right. He had a lot of money too." Tasha is curios, "What happened to him?" Tawana says jokingly, "I shot him." They all began to laugh. "Now, I'm not afraid of a gun anymore and I owe it all to him." The ladies are putting on leather gloves. Amura talks with a serious tone of voice, "O.K. enough of the bullshit." Everyone stops laughing. "Tawana you stay your ass down here. The rest of us are going up stairs to get this motherfucker and hope that the money is up there too. The motherfucker is on the 5th floor. 5-E to be exact. Everybody got there gloves on." Amura's steps out of the utility van into a puddle of water. Everyone else in the car all get out also. All four of them walk across the street to the hotel in the rain. All four of them walk in the hotel. The same short fat white male that had confrontation with Dt. Jadean, he is sitting behind the desk. He nods his head. Amura just blows a kiss at him. The women walk straight to the elevator. Amura presses the 5th button. The door closes. All of the women stand quiet. The elevator door opens and all four of the women walk out of the elevator. There is a sign showing the direction of the all apartments. They all walk down to the apartment at the end of the hall. They are looking at the apartment door numbers and letters. Spanish Fly pulls out a knife from her trench coat. Spanish music is being played from the room and laughing loud. Amura says, "5-E. Ain't this something? I see someone is having a good time. Fly pick the lock." Spanish Fly digs the knife between the lock and the steel. She then bumps the door with her shoulder. The door opens. They walk into the room and the lights are off except the lamp on the nightstand. Light from the window lights the room. The music is louder since they all came in. Ricky is in the shower. The steam from the shower blows in the room a head. A Latino woman is sitting on the bed with her back turned to the women. The Latino woman sitting on the bed bends over to sniff some coke that is on the nightstand. She then falls back on the bed with her eyes close. The woman shouts, "Ricky, are you ready to do it again." She opens her eyes and she is frightened by the reflection of her face in the knife. The knife is by the woman's right cheek. The woman screams and Spanish Fly immediately covers her mouth. Spanish

Fly slaps her. Spanish Fly whispers, "Be quiet or I will cut your throat senorita. Sit the fuck up. The woman sits up in the bed. "What did he do?" Amura says, "You'll soon find out, just sit there and be real quiet and you won't get your pretty face cut up. O.K.!" Spanish Fly says, "And, I do it real good mommy, so I think you should take her advice!" Precious Jewell says, "Should we go in and get him?" Amura responds, "No let's wait for his spic pretty boy ass to come out." Inside the bathroom, there is a small Latino man in the shower. His name is Ricky. Ricky is dancing to the Spanish music in the shower. The sound of the music is turned down. Ricky shouts, " Mommy what happened to the music, are you ready for your knight in shinning armor to come lick that tasty pussy some more. Huh! The Latino woman shouts "Oh yes papi!" Precious Jewell has a gun with a silencer pointed to the woman's head. In the bathroom Ricky throws on a bathrobe and shouts, "Here I come my little Spanish Fly." Ricky walks out of the bathroom. Spanish Fly is at the side of the door. As soon as he walk out of the bathroom, Spanish Fly punches him in the face. He falls to the floor. Spanish Fly shouts, "You got the wrong one mutherfucker. It's only one Spanish Fly Ricky." Amura and Tasha draw their guns with silencers at Ricky. Precious Jewell still has the gun pointed to the woman's head. Ricky is on the floor with his mouth busted open. Amura says, "How are you doing Ricky? I see you having a good time." "Not anymore, now that you're here." Spanish Fly kicks him again. Amura smiles and says, " Ricky, Ricky are you getting Alzheimer's disease Ricky. You know we can play this game all day, but unfortunately we don't have the time or the fucken patience. So where's the money." "I spent it." Amura barks, "What the fuck you mean you spent it? You just got it a week ago and you were supposed to bring it straight to us. So stop playing, give us the money." "It's right there in the suitcase by the bed." He points in the direction of the suitcase. Tasha goes to pick up the suitcase. She opens it on the bed. "Goddamn, I can see that it is about 100,000 short. What the fuck you did with it Ricky?" Amura says, "We want answers Ricky. Bigtime is gonna ask me what happened to that fucking money. And if I have to hear it, your ear is gonna be right in my pocket to hear it too. Get it? Spanish Fly puts the knife to Ricky's ear. Ricky says," All right, I went to Atlantic City and I lost it O.K. Mommy please don't cut off my ear, I need these things. My face just wouldn't look right." Spanish Fly says with anger, "Get your ass up on the bed, you asshole." Spanish Fly sticks the knife in Ricky's ear. Ricky gets off of the floor to go sit on the bed right next to the woman. Precious Jewell still has the gun pointed at the woman. Spanish Fly grabs the woman by the hair. "Damn Ricky, you have good taste. Being that you're Latino, I know you ate her pussy. It is spicy or sweet." Amura says, "Ricky, I really don't know what your problem is, but this isn't gonna happen again." Ricky says, "No senorita, it isn't. I promise. I'm good people, you know I'll make it up to you. I'll get your money back." Amura laughs. "I know because where gonna fuck you up. Where going to take your finger nails off." She laughs. "I'm just fucking with you. You know why it's not a problem, because I know you get money. But first, let me go to the bathroom. We will talk Ricky." Amura walks to the bathroom. Spanish Fly puts her knife back in her knife holster. Precious Jewell and Tasha draw their guns down. Spanish Fly says, "Ay Ricky got any wine." Ricky points to the table. It is two 40-ounce malt liquor bottles of Colt 45 and some cheap wine. "Over there." Spanish Fly walks over to the table. Spanish Fly says, "What the fuck is this? You are not Billy Dee Williams. You took over 300,000 thousand dollars and you got this shit. Spanish Fly looks at Precious Jewell. "You want Jewell?" Precious Jewell respond with a nasty attitude. "It's Precious." "Ooh, little feisty are we. That's uncommon for someone that just came into this crew. You saw what happened to the last bitch you killed." "Do you want to be the next bitch?" Inside the bathroom, Amura is on the toilet taking her maxi pad off. It is bloody. She slides it in the toilet through her legs. She has another in her pocket. She reaches for it. Amura shouts, "Tasha tells Tawana we are coming down." Tasha closes the suitcase of money. She then paces the room. She takes out her cellular phone and dials Tawana's number. Tawana is in the van smoking marijuana and the van is fogged up. Her phone rings. She answers the phone. "What's the deal? Y'all on the way down." I got the van running." She hangs up. Tasha turns the phone off and puts it in her pocket. Ricky and the woman are looking like they are up to something. Precious Jewell and Spanish Fly are staring at one another. Tasha shouts, "Everything is everything." Amura is still on the toilet. Amura shouts, "All right. I think it was the cheese I ate last night. I got my period and I had to take a shit. She is wiping her ass. Precious Jewell and Spanish Fly are staring at one another. Precious Jewell says, "What's your problem anyway, you have something against me." I'm here with you right." Spanish Fly replies, "I was just joking with you. Bitch!" "Who you calling a bitch?" "I'm calling you a bitch. You know what, what the fuck you wanna do?" Tasha shouts, "All right, cut it out, the both of you." Spanish Fly and Precious Jewell both approach one another and are still arguing. Ricky whispers to the woman. "Open the draw, there is a gun." Ricky nods his head to the woman. The woman reaches over to the nightstand and opens it and grabs the gun and it has a silencer on it and begins to shoot. She fires one shot at Tasha and grazes her neck. Tasha falls to the floor. Spanish Fly and Precious Jewell splits apart and runs for cover. The woman continues to pulls the trigger shooting, there are no more bullets in the gun. Ricky runs toward the door and opens the door. Precious Jewell shoots Ricky in the back of his head. The blood splatters all over the door. Ricky falls on the floor. Spanish Fly walks over to the woman and cuts her throat. The woman's blood drips all over the bed. Spanish Fly lets her fall face down in the bed. Tasha gets off of the floor holding her neck. Amura steps out of the bathroom and says, "Where the fuck is Ricky?" Amura looks to the door. "Oh, the motherfucker is dead. Let's get the fuck out of here." The women leave out of the hotel room in a hurry. They all run down the hallway to the stairs. They run down the stairs that leads to the lobby of the building. Amura blows a kiss to the owner of the building. He smiles and blows a kiss back. Outside the apartment building. The women are all walking back to the car in the rain. Tasha has the suitcase of cash and is holding her neck. Amura says, "That never ever happens again. If you have a problem, keep that outside what we have to do. Tasha are you all right." "Shit I'm fine. Luckily the bitch graze my neck, or I be haunting you motherfuckers in your dreams." They all get in the utility van. Tawana is already behind the drivers' seat. The women are in the van. Tawana pulls off into traffic. The utility van drives down the street. The women are all settled in the car. Tawana says, "Did you get the money?" Amura replied, "It is short probably about 100,000." Tawana looks at Tasha by looking at the rare view mirror. "Tasha, what happen to you?" Tasha barks, "What the fuck it looks like? I got shot in my neck." Amura turns around in the car seat and smacks Precious Jewell in the face. Precious Jewell looks in shock. Precious Jewell is about to say something and Amura pulls out her gun and says, "What bitch, I run this crew and you fucked up. I heard what you said. Call me Precious, what type of bullshit is that. Don't let that shit happen again. You hear me." Precious Jewell looks at Amura, shaking her head yes. Amura turns around and sits in the seat. "So what did you do with that guy the other night?" Amura pulls down the mirror from the sun visor. Precious Jewell says, "He just drove me home. That's all". Amura and Precious Jewell make eye contact when Amura looks through the mirror at Precious Jewell.

Later on that night.
Tawana, Amura, Spanish Fly, and Tasha are leaving out of the office. Precious Jewell is sitting down at the round table counting money. Amura says, "Precious don't forget to lock the safe. I'll see you when I get back from Africa. I'll be there for about two weeks. Spanish Fly shouts, "Yeah bitch, you heard that." Amura looks at Spanish Fly, "There you go with the bullshit." Spanish Fly answer back, "I'm not worried about you smacking me or pulling out a gun on me." "Fuck you." The women leave out of the office. Tawana is last slamming the door. Precious Jewell finish counting the money. She grabs the money and walks over to the save. She puts the money in the safe. She slams the safe. She walks back to the table. Precious Jewell picks up her cellular phone off of the table and dials Dt. Steele's number and puts the phone to her ear. Dt. Steele is across down at a murder investigation. The room is filled with investigating officers. They are investigating the dead bodies. It is Ricky and the woman. Ricky is laying dead in the door entrance and the woman dead in the bed from her throat being slashed. Blood is all over the bed. The camera flash flashes light in the room. Dt. Steele and Dt. Jadean are looking at the dead body on the floor the bullet hole in the door . "The man has a gun shot wound to the head." Dt Steele says, "Damn, that shit went straight through his head. I want to know what this

was all about?" Dt. Jadean responds, "I arrested this guy before. He had a broken gun. Dt. Steele phone rings. He goes in his jacket pocket and pulls out the phone and answers it. Dt. Steele, "Who is it?" Precious Jewell voice can be heard over the phone. "It's Precious, baby what's up?" "I can't talk right now, I'll speak to you later." Dt. Steele clicks his phone off. "Are there any cameras around?" He looks at Dt. Jadean. Back at the office, "Precious Jewell clicks off here phone and drops it on the table. The door slams. Marquis has just stepped inside the office. "So where the fuck you been?" Marquis walks over to Precious Jewell. Marquis responds, "I been handling business across seas and getting my dick suck. So what's up with you? Precious Jewell shakes her head looking sad, "I was trying to call somebody, but they are busy right now. I'll call them later". "You want to get high." Your sister told me that you shoot up." "I don't have a problem with it." "Neither do I. I shot crystal meth before, but never heroin. What's up, I'm game for anything?" Marquis smiles and says, "I got some shit from East Africa. You should see how beautiful the field's look. It is not to far from the ocean. I have a whole new set up. I didn't even tell Amura about it yet. I don't want her to slap me in my face and give me a lecture about it. And the bitch has the nerves to pull out a gun on me." Marquis digs in his pocket and bulls out a syringe and a few ounces of heroin in a plastic zip lock bag and drops it on the table. He digs in his back pocket and pulls out a spoon. He bends the spoon back so it can stand by on it's own. Marquis takes off his jacket and puts it on the chair. He rolls his shirtsleeve up. He sits down at the table. Marquis bends the spoon so that it could stand up by itself. He reaches for the liquor on the table. He opens the liquor and pours a little inside the spoon. "You want some? You wanna test out the new product? What you wanna do?" Marquis reaches for the zip lock bag of heroin. He opens the bag and digs in to get a pinch of the heroin. He drops it in the spoon with the liquor in it. He reaches in his pocket to get his lighter. He flicks his lighter and it shoots out fire like a blowtorch. He moves the lighter under the spoon. The spoon gets hot, and the liquor and heroin comes to a boil. Marquis moves the lighter from under the spoon. Marquis says, "Take the syringe out of the pack." Precious Jewell reaches on the table to take the needle out of the pack. "Pass me the syringe." She passes Marquis the syringe. Marquis sticks the needle into the heroin and sucks it into the syringe. "Are you down to test this shit with me, right now? This shit right her could make a hundred mil guaranteed. All I need is a partner. And we don't have to kill nobody unless it is needed. Not like those stupid bitches that follow my sister. My sister is a foul bitch. She let your cousin Sheeka go down. Sheeka didn't have to that bid by herself. Amura was there too. Enough of that shit, are you down." "Down with what?" "Shooting this shit in my arm or making a hundred million with out your sister." Marquis replies, "Both! "They don't believe me anyway. Don't fucking run your mouth about this O.K." "O.K." She smiles. "Take your belt off." "That's all right, I went to the store and brought phone wire. Yo, you did this before." "I just didn't do it in about a year. I usually shoot up in my leg. I don't want people to see track marks in my arm. Fuck it! It's a first time for everything." He digs in his jacket pocket and pulls out three pieces of phone wire. He throws it on the table and Marquis and Precious tie the phone wire around each other arms. Then she begins to tap her arm with two fingers to get a vein to pop up. Marquis does the same thing. Precious Jewell says, "I use to watch my mother and father shoot up." Marquis reaches for the syringe and injects the heroin into his arm. Some of his blood goes into the syringe. He passes it to Precious Jewell. Marquis closes his eyes feeling the rush. Precious Jewell sticks herself in the arm. Marquis's blood along with the heroin is injected into Precious Jewell's vein she feels it and closes her eyes.

CHAPTER 6
SHE TOLD

Precious Jewell and her cousin Sheeka are walking down the street talking. They are walking down the street with there shopping bags. Sheeka says, "So what up Precious, you that bitch now?" Precious Jewell snaps, "What you talking about? I always been that bitch. Where you been?" It's been about a year." "I was in fucking jail, you remember bitch." Precious Jewell giggles. "Who you think you talking to?" Precious Jewell stops walking. Sheeka stops also. "Where you been, and who the fuck you been with. Didn't I tell you to stay away from that club?" Sheeka gets in Precious Jewell's face. They both drop their shopping bags. She slaps Precious Jewell real hard in the face. Precious Jewell stares at Sheeka. "Why didn't you do that shit to Amura? You did do 7 years in jail for her, remember." "Oh so you been with Amura huh? I heard about you. Your heart pumps blood now." Sheeka swings at Precious Jewell again and Precious Jewell grabs her hand and pulls a razor to Sheeka's throat. Precious Jewell says, "Don't do it again." Precious Jewell picks her bags off of the floor. She flags for a cab. Sheeka shouts, "Don't call me when your ass get in trouble." A cab driver stops for Precious Jewell then pulls off. It is the same cab driver that picked her up from the airport." A car pulls up and starts to take pictures of Precious Jewell and Sheeka arguing. Click, Click. Click, Click, Click, Click, Click. Pictures are taken of them. Another cab stops and picks up Precious Jewell. Precious Jewell gets into the cab. She sticks her middle finger out the window at Sheeka. Sheeka says, "You know where I'm at. You will come crawling back." The camera takes pictures of Precious Jewell middle finger. Click, Click.

15 minutes later.

The taxicab pulls up slowly to the curb. Precious Jewell gets out of the cab. People are walking on the crowded sidewalk. There is an African woman standing in front of a newsstand. Precious Jewell approaches her and says, "I saw the way you were looking at me when my people and your people made the deal." Mamadou says, "Yeah, when I'm here in America I live the life. If I were back home in

Africa, they would cut my clitoris off if they found out that I love women. Precious Jewell replies, "I just got into it. Amura brought me into the life. She is the only woman I had sex with." Mamadou smiles, "Amura is the one who brought me into the life. Let's go back to my hotel and we can talk some more and talk about business. Marquis said I could trust you." "Yes you can." A hand with gloves sticks outside the window of a car with a camera taking pictures. Click, Click, Click the sound of the camera taking pictures of Precious Jewell and Mamadou. Precious Jewell and Mamadou begin to kiss. As they are kissing, the camera is taking pictures of them kissing.

Early the next morning.
The music of Anita Baker's "Caught In The Rapture", roses are all over the hotel room. Dt. Steele and Precious Jewell enter the hotel room. Dt. Steele has blind folded Precious Jewell eyes so that she cannot see the roses that are around the room. He grabs her hand and leads her in. Dt. Steele says, "Come on in here." Dt Steele leads Precious Jewell to the bed. Precious Jewell, "Steele, come on. Let me see." "O.K. baby girl." Dt. Steele takes the blindfold off of her face. Precious Jewell is in ore with

what she sees. Her eyes began to get watery. "No man or nobody has never made me feel so good and happy." Precious Jewell hugs him and they began to kiss passionately. They take their clothing off in lust." Dt. Steele pulls out a condom.

★★★

2 hours later.

Precious Jewell and Dt. Steele are lying in the bed looking at the ceiling. Both are smoking a cigarette. Precious Jewell turns her head looking at Dt. Steele. Precious Jewell says, "Steele, I know something." "Call me Omar. What are you talking about?" "I know who been doing the killings to the murders you are investigating." Flashes of the murders runs across Precious Jewell's mind as she talks. Dt. Steele replies, "What are you talking about, what murders?" "The first time we met, I went through those pictures" Precious Jewell gets memory flashes of the murders. "The woman with the bullet to the left eye, I was there. The woman head blown off, I was there." "So who are behind the murders?" Precious Jewell answers, "Amura to name a few. She's in Africa right now. I'll tell you everything if you promise me immunity and protection. All of the murders are apart of an International drug cartel. From Africa to L.A then here to New York. All of the murders are drug related. Please baby don't let them get." Dt Steele answers back with compassion, "I promise I will not let anything happen to you. I'm in love with you. I'll get a search warrant and I'll make sure arrest will be made. Better yet after all this is over, why don't you come to Amsterdam with me?" Dt. Steele kindly strokes his hands through Precious Jewell's hair. They both hug one another. Precious Jewell says, "I love you Omar."

In East Africa

The sun is shining and it is hot day in Africa. The wind blows the sand in the air. An African General of the Army is driving the jeep with Amura and Tawana sitting as passengers. Amura is sitting in the front and Tawana sitting in the back. The wind blows their hair. The jeep rides down the dirt road. The dust from the sand flies in the air from the tire tracks. The jeep enters a small African village; armed soldiers stand guard with people walking and children playing. They are being watched by every one as they enter the village. The top general of the army of the African country is looking out the window at them from his office. He has his soldiers stand guard in the room with him. The office a apart of a beautiful palace. He sees the jeep pulling to a stop. Amura,

Tawana, and the Army Lt. General gets out of the jeep. Inside the office, General Imean walks over to the table to sit in his chair. He opens the draw to get a cigar and he light's it and he begins to smoke. "Cuban cigars are the best." Amura, Tawana, and the Army Lt. General Fatai walk into the office. General Imean tells his soldiers in his native language to leave. He says to Amura and Tawana, "How was your trip here?" Amura responds, "It was fine. It is very hot here." General Imean smiles and says, "Yes, my people are the people of the sun." Amura barks, "Let's get down to business. What is the fucking problem with you slowing down the shipments?" "I hear that you are making a lot of money in America. I want some more money on this table. I want a cut in on the action. My people are taken the bigger risk. What if they die from mulling that heroin into your country.? You know soon there will be a cure of the AIDS virus, then what would you do. You are getting the purest heroin in the world and you are able to step on it and make a lot of money." The General nods his head at the Lt. General. The Lt. General pulls out his gun from the holster. Amura and Tawana look at him. Amura shouts, "Mr. Fatai, you are scientist, do you know Mr. Imean's family allowed those scientist from Europe and the United States to inject the people in this village with the SV40 simian virus which was used in the polio vaccines in the 1960's. This bastard's family helped jump start the AIDS virus. Do you want his job? I'll cut you in on the action." She turns to the general and she points to him. "Shoot that motherfucker. The Lt. General walks over and shoots the General Imean in the head. Boom! The general's brain is all over the place. The soldiers run in with there guns drawn. The general is dead sitting in the chair with a bullet hole in the head and his brains are all over the place. The Lt. General tells the soldiers that he is now in charge. Lt. General Fatal says to the ladies, "I'll speed up the shipments," he pauses, "and by the way." the Lt. General turns around and smiles, "when will I'll see the money?"

★★★

The next day
It is a hot sunny afternoon and the sun is setting. Amura and Tawana are lying under the umbrella in their bikinis outside the Presidential Palace that faces the ocean. They are on a beautiful beach front with the new Army General. General Fatai is giving Amura a foot massage. They are lying next to a pool. A female servant brings them drinks and a cellular phone. Amura picks the phone off of the silver platter and Tawana takes the drinks. Amura puts the phone to her ear. Amura responds to the message, "What the fuck! What?" She looks surprised the anger

comes over her. She is receiving a message from Bigtime. She puts the phone on speaker. Bigtime says, "You need to come out here." A cough is heard over the speaker. "We got a problem. Some one in your crew done ran their mouth. So you better handle it." General Fatai stops rubbing Amura's feet

and is listening to the conversation. Tawana is drinking from both glasses she took off the platter. Tawana is untroubled my the conversation. "Amura here. Take your drink." Amura reaches for her drink. Amura asks, "Bigtime who is it?" A cough is heard over the speaker. "That new bitch you've brought in. That bitch you fucking." "Bigtime are you sure? Not Precious?" "Cancel that bitch. I'll see you in New York." The phone clicks. Amura clicks the phone off. She lookes at Tawana in disbelieve shaking her head from side to side. Amura says, "We got to go back to New York. That bitch done ran her mouth and we got to go plug that bitch." Tawana responds, "Let's enjoy our stay. When we get back to the states, we will handle that.

PERFECT PAIR
PUBLICATIONS

CHAPTER 7

KILL HER

3 days later at Marquis house in the afternoon, music can be heard down the hallway "Whoodni's 5 Minutes Of Funk". Down the hall, sunlight lights the room. Marquis is sitting on the couch in the living room smoking marijuana. The marijuana smoke fills the air. The phone rings. Ring! Ring! Ring! Marquis reaches for the phone and he knocks it down on the floor. He reaches to the floor to pick up the phone, and then he sits back down. Marquis shouts, "Yo! Who the fuck is this?" It is Tawana and Amura at the air port. They are walking out of the airport. Tawana is on her cell phone at the airport. Tawana says, "Marquis turn the damn music down!" Marquis grabs the remote control turning the music down. Marquis says, "What the fuck? Who are we going to kill now? Because I'm not doing shit." Tawana replied,"

Marquis you must be high right now. Shit, talk to your sister." Tawana passes Amura the phone. Amura looks at Tawana shaking her head. She slowly puts her ear to the phone. Amura says, "Listen, I don't have time for the bullshit. We have to take care of business." "Who the fuck are we killing? Who are we going to kill now? Marquis shouts. Amura shouts back, "You know what motherfucker, we got to make a stop. We will be there in 2 hours. Marquis call Spanish Fly and Tasha." "What about Precious?" "You heard what the fuck I said? I thought so!" Amura hangs the phone on Marquis. "Tawana you got all the bags." Tawana holds her Gucci handbag up to Amura. "Yeah! Let's go." They exit out of the airport onto the street.

2 hour later at Marquis House.
Spanish Fly and Tasha are standing at Marquis's door pushing and shoving one another. They both knock on the door. Spanish Fly says, "Damn would you stop! You know Marquis got two bathrooms." Tasha replied, "And you know that one of the toilets is working. The last time I was here, that toilet had backed-up shit. It was the worst fucking smell I have smelled in my life, and you know I been around a lot of dead bodies. Marquis opens the door and the both of them run into the apartment. Marquis

closes the door. Marquis is looking at the Tasha and Spanish Fly as they run down the hall. Marquis is watching the both of them argue. As he walks up the hallway. They are pushing and shoving one another. Marquis says, "Tasha I fixed it already." Tasha and Spanish Fly stopped shoving and pushing. Tasha shouts, "I can't remember which one it was." Tasha and Spanish Fly are looking at both of the bathrooms. Both of the doors are closed. One in front of them and the other one down the hall. Marquis tells Tasha, "Tasha it was this bathroom right there." Marquis points to the bathroom. Tasha runs to the other bathroom. Spanish Fly walks to the other bathroom. Spanish Fly shakes her head. "Fly this is the bathroom that doesn't have the fucked-up toilet. Baby girl you know I like you ,fuck Tasha." Spanish Fly pulls her panties down and sits on the toilet. Tasha is yelling down the hall at Marquis. "You fucking bastard." "Tasha is walking back down the hallway to the living room." Tasha walks in the living room. "Why didn't you fix the fucking toilet? I didn't have to use the bathroom anyway. Pass me the weed motherfucker." She walks toward Marquis and he passes her the marijuana. She puts it to her lips. She inhales the marijuana. "Damn, this is some good fucking weed." She exhales and coughs. She inhales again. She blows the smoke in the air. Spanish Fly comes out of the bathroom and says, "Pass the weed, Yo Marquis, You got the old Snoop Dog shit. That old Death Row shit." "I got that shit." He grabs the remote control off the table to turn up the volume and starts play Snoop Dogg's "Gin and Juice", they all begin to sing to the song. He puts the remote back on the table." Boom! Boom! Boom! They all turn to the door! It is Amura and Tawana. They are standing at the door. Amura says, "I know them motherfuckers heard us knocking." She bangs on the door harder. Marquis opens the door. There is a chain on the door leaving it half-open. Marquis puts his face between the opening. Amura and Marquis make eye contact and says, "What is the password?" "Stop fucking playing with me Marquis." Amura roars. Marquis closes the door and removes the chain from the door. He opens the door. "Open the door." Amura and Tawana shake their heads walking into the apartment. Tawana stops and she looks at Marquis, she acts like she is going to hit Marquis. Marquis jerks his body from getting hit. Marquis says, "Bitch! Fuck you." Marquis slams the door. He yells down the hall. "Pass the weed." Amura and Tawana walks into the living room dancing to the beat of the song "Gin and Juice". The air is filled with smoke from the marijuana. Amura coughs. Amura says, "Pass the herb. Let me hit that dirty ho." Spanish Fly passes Amura the marijuana. Amura takes a heavy intake. Amura blows the smoke out of her nose. Amura passes the marijuana back to Spanish Fly. Amura yells, "Turn the motherfuckin' music down." Marquis, turn that motherfucker down." Marquis picks the remote off of the table and turns the volume down. He puts the remote back on the table. "We got a fucking problem. I see my little bitch been running her fucking mouth to the cops." Marquis howls back, "Who the fuck told you that? I know Precious would not do anything like that." Amura gets up in Marquis's face, How you know Marquis? Amura stares at Marquis. "Well, Bigtime told me. She said something about those fucking murders." Marquis is shaking his head walking toward the couch. "It looks like we both lost on that bet." Marquis begins to cry. "I can't take it any more. I can't see you kill another and me taking part in that motherfucker. Do you have love for life?" Amura shouts, "Yes the fuck I do. I give a fuck about your life." "What the fuck you mean you give a fuck about my life?" Amura says calmly, "Your ass is dying?" "What?" That bitch we set on fire, that bitch you was shooting with, that bitch, she had H.I.V. Marquis. "You bullshitting me." "It is the truth. She had H.I.V., and the bitch knew about it. The bitch gave a motherfucker who begs for money on the street H.I.V. That's why I wanted that bitch to watch herself burn to death. Amura walks over to Marquis. She goes to hugs him. Marquis pushes her arms away. He walks pass Spanish Fly. Marquis looks at her and shakes his head. Everyone else in the room are in shock. "Marquis I didn't know how to tell you. You know how motherfuckers talk. But a few people I know that you shoot-up with are in the hospital laying up in a plastic bubble. They got AIDS. The medicine that they were taken no longer works for them. Before I came here I had to go to the hospital to see it for my self. So Marquis, we can pull together with this baby. We can get you the best doctors and the best medication if it's all true. You need to get tested." Marquis sits on the couch., "Why you did not tell me this back then Amura its been almost a year." "Baby, I told you to be careful." Marquis shakes his head. "That's fucked up. I don't even care. Precious was shooting that shit with me too. Truthfully I know that I should have used my own needles and should have used condoms. I went to the Department of Health to get checked and my result was positive yesterday. I guess God don't like ugly. Shit we got people with AIDS in Africa transporting heroin for us." Maybe I can get the Magic Johnson treatment where my viral load is low. But then again, every human body is different. He pauses. Amura I still could have been the biggest drug dealer in the world if I would have finish school. I could have made a vaccine to fight H.I.V." Marquis right hand is resting on the couch, he reaches for the gun behind the pillow. He grabs the gun holding it behind the pillow. No one knows that he has his hand on the gun. "My eyes grow weary of the sun, Amura. From a child, I saw my mother kill and now my sister." Marquis laughs. " Precious needs to get her self checked out. I know for sure she got it, my blood got into the syringe we shared. Just the fear of me knowing I got this shit is going to kill me." Marquis puts the gun to his head. He takes the safety of the gun. Amura shouts, "Put that fucking gun down, now. You hear me" Amura runs towards Marquis screaming. "No! No! Marquis don't do it." Boom! Marquis falls back in the couch. His brains are on the couch and on the floor. Amura grabs him and hugs him. All of the ladies walks over and hugs Marquis and Amura. Fly, Tasha go to that bitch house and Tawana go to Sheeka's house. I'll handle Marquis." She cries. "Baby boy, why did you have to do this to yourself." Spanish Fly, Tasha, and Tawana walk out of the room to make their exit out of the apartment. Amura's lays Marquis body back on the couch. Ring, Ring, Ring, is the sound from the phone. Amura picks up the phone. "Bigtime your brother killed himself. He just blew his fucking brains out." A voice comes over the phone. A cough is heard. "Oh God no, not my brother. You got to take care of Precious, we'll take care of Marquis's his finger prints game up. I'll be there." "All right!"

★★★

2 Hours Later

Inside Precious Jewell apartment. Precious Jewell is standing in the window smoking a cigarette. She opens the window blinds and the light from the streetlight shines in her face. She looks at the parked car that is outside. The streetlight is shining on the car. The car door opens. Spanish Fly and Tasha get out of the car. Precious Jewell is in the window smoking a cigarette. She exhales the smoke onto the glass. The smoke fills the air between her and the window. Precious Jewell says to herself, "What the fuck they doing here? They would usually call before coming. It must be important. Let me open the door before I go to the bathroom." Precious walks to the door to unlock it. She cracks open the door. She goes to the bathroom. Spanish Fly and Tasha are walking across the street talking. Tasha says to Spanish Fly, "We let this bitch join the click and this is our payback." Spanish Fly responds, "I'm going to kick that bitch dead in the face with my heel." There is man walking across the street staring at Tasha. They approach one another on the sidewalk. The man name is Justin. He says, "What's up Tasha, what's up Fly?" Tasha smiles at Justin, "Yo, when you got out of rehab." "About mouth ago. But I got AIDS. That bitch Kima gave it to me. I heard that bitch got set on fire. That's good for that bitch." Tasha puts on a phony look on her face, she playing like she is shocked from what she heard, "Get out of here. When did you hear that?" Spanish Fly says, "I'm going to go up stairs." She goes in her jacket pocket and pulls out some brass knuckles. She puts them on her hand. She put her hand on the knife that is on the side of her hip. She opens the door and she begins to walk up the stairs. Tasha and the man are talking. Tasha says, "Get out of here, they still didn't find who burned that girl like that." Spanish Fly gets to Precious Jewell door. Spanish Fly knocks on the door. The door slowly opens. Spanish Fly slowly walks inside the apartment then closing the door. Spanish Fly shouts, "Precious are you here!" Precious Jewell is in the bathroom wiping her face with a washcloth. She is giggling. She gets silent and puts her ear to the door. Spanish Fly takes a knife from her hip. Precious Jewell has her ear to the door. She touches the door. The door squeaks. Spanish Fly looks in the direction of the door. She walks slowly to the bathroom. Spanish Fy says, "Damn I can't believe this bitch is not here. Most of all I can't believe this bitch ran her mouth. Precious Jewell stands in the bathroom looking shocked. Spanish Fly yells, "You fucking bitch! A knife comes through the bathroom door. Spanish Fly pulls the knife out of the door. Precious Jewell falls to the floor. Spanish Fly kicks the door open. Precious Jewell yells, "What the fuck is going on?" "You ran your fucking mouth rite?" Precious Jewell replies, "I don't know what you are talking about." Precious pulls herself up by grabbing the bathtub. Spanish Fly swings with the knife. Precious Jewell backs away and tackles Spanish Fly to the floor out of the bathroom into the living room area. The knife falls out of Spanish Fly's hand. Precious Jewell is on top of Spanish Fly punching her in the face. Precious Jewell says, "What the fuck is wrong with you?" "Bitch you know what you did? Get the fuck off of me." Spanish Fly flips Precious Jewell over on the floor. Spanish Fly gets off the floor quickly. She runs over and kicks Precious Jewell in the face. Precious Jewell falls on the floor. Precious Jewell tries to get up of the floor. Spanish Fly punches Precious Jewell in her face with the brass knuckles. Precious Jewell falls on the floor face first. Precious Jewell has a busted lip. Spanish Fly kicks her in the back with the heel of her shoe. Precious Jewell screams in pain. Spanish Fly says, "Yeah bitch, you fucked up." Precious Jewell turns her body over she is dizzy from getting hit in the face She drags herself away from Spanish Fly. Precious Jewell, "I don't believe a word you have just said. Bitch you probably fucked up on some money and you are telling Amura I did it. Wait till I tell Amura. Spanish Fly is walking over toward Precious Jewell. Precious Jewell turns her head slightly to the right and she sees a syringe with heroin in it. Spanish Fly kneels down. She grabs Precious Jewell shirt collar and says, "You got a lot of fucking nerves." Precious Jewell reaches for the syringe. Precious Jewell spits in Spanish Fly's face. "No, you have a lot of fucking nerves, bitch." Precious Jewell stabs Spanish Fly with the needle in her throat, pressing down on the top of the syringe injecting the heroin in Spanish Fly's neck. Precious Jewell gets up off the floor. Spanish Fly is screaming. Spanish Fly charges Precious Jewell. Precious Jewell moves out of the way, then pushing Spanish Fly out of the window. Spanish Fly crashes out of the window 4 stories down. Tasha and the man see Spanish Fly's body fall from the 4th floor. Glass from the window is falling also. Tasha and the man move out of the way just in time. Spanish Fly's body hits the ground very hard. Her head is busted open bleeding on the sidewalk. The syringe is still sticking in her neck. Tasha bends down looking at Spanish Fly's body. Tasha shakes her head then she turns her head looking up at the 4th floor window and Precious Jewell sticks her head out the window. Tasha yells, " Precious, you fucking bitch." Tasha pulls out under her trench coat, a Mac 11 automatic. She runs inside the building. The man who is standing there with Tasha goes inside Spanish Fly's coat pocket taking out money and then running down the street. Justin says, "I'm going to get high right now." Tasha runs up the stairs with her gun drawn. Precious Jewell is running around the apartment grabbing her coat, putting on her shoes and the gun on the bookstand. She then makes her way toward the window with the fire escape. She opens the window and slides out of the window. She climbs up the fire escape. Tasha busts through the door with a Mac. 11 shooting the whole entire room. She turns to the window and sees Precious Jewell's feet climbing the fire escape. She shoots through the window barely missing Precious Jewell. Tasha runs to the window looking out of it seeing Precious Jewell making it to the top of the building. The sound of a door squeaking gets Tasha's attention. It is the African woman who Precious Jewell met. Mamadou has a phone wire wrapped around her arm and a syringe sticking in her arm. The woman is so fucking high she doesn't know what is going on. Tasha recognizes here. Tasha says, "Mamadou, what the fuck you doing here? Fuck it." Tasha shoots Mamadou with rest of the bullets that was left in the gun. Mamadou fall to the floor. Tasha takes the clip out of the gun and puts the clip in her pocket and pulls out another and injects it into the gun. She walks over and shoots Mamadou in the face. Tasha runs out of the apartment. Precious Jewell is running across the roof to get away from Tasha. She jumps to the next roof. Tasha bust through the door on the roof just missing Precious Jewell. Tasha runs across the roof looking for Precious Jewell. Tasha gets to the edge and sees her and begins to shoot the Mac. 11 at Precious Jewell. Precious Jewell runs across the roof not getting hit. Dt. Jadean is riding in the car by himself. On the walkie-talkie a female gives a report about shots being fire. Police dispatcher says, "Shots are being fired on Mann St. and 5th. The call said it is a woman shooting a big gun." Dt. Jadean speeds off to the scene of the shooting. Precious Jewell climbs down another fire escape that leads to an alleyway. Tasha hears the cops coming from the roof and she then runs back through the roof door. Precious Jewell is running down the alleyway. As soon as she gets out of the alleyway the cops turn the corner. Tasha runs out of the building with her hands inside her jacket holding the gun. People are standing around looking at Spanish Fly's body. The cops' roll up to the curb and jumps out of their squad car. The cops says, "Every body back up. Where were those shots being fired?" An old lady points to Tasha. The old lady says, "Ask that bitch right there, I saw her run inside that building with a big fucking gun. The cops turn to Tasha. "Do you know anything about that?" The cop sees a bulge in Tasha's coat. The cops make and attempt for their guns and yells, "Drop the gun." "Fuck that!" Tasha shouts.

Tasha draws her gun and begins to shoot at the cops. She sprays everyone standing in front of her. She shoots the cops and all the bystanders standing there. Every one began to scream on the street bleeding from the gun shoots. Tasha runs across the street to the car. She sees Precious Jewell down the block standing on the corner sticking her middle finger up at Tasha. Precious Jewell is standing at the corner looking at Tasha. Precious Jewell yells down the street, "Fuck you bitch." Tasha shoots at Precious Jewell. Dt. Jadean is tiptoeing right up from behind with his gun drawn. He puts the gun to Tasha's head and says, "Freeze! Put that motherfuckin gun on the floor. Better yet bitch you get on the floor." Tasha drops the gun. She turns very slowly looking at Dt. Jadean through the corner of her eyes. She grabs his risk with the gun and bends it around and the gun goes off shooting Tasha on the side. She screams in agony. She breaks his risk and takes the gun out off his hand. She punches him in the nose bone. He grabs his nose while the blood flows though his fingers. Tasha shots him in the face. She picks up her Mac.11 and shoots his body numerous times. She puts Dt. Jadean's gun on her waistline. She grabs her side. Tasha runs to the car holding her side she is in so much pain. She gets in and starts the car and pulls off. Tasha says, "Y'all motherfuckers got to kill me." Police cars turn the corner. People are screaming pointing in the direction of the speeding car Tasha is in.

★★★

Across Town At Sheeka's House

Sheeka is sitting in the living room smoking a joint listening to music. She picks up the wine glass and walks out of the living room. Sheeka walks into the kitchen. She walks over to the table and pours wine into the glass. The sound of a mouse catches Sheeka's attention. Squeak, squeak, squeak, squeak. Sheeka turns around and walks over to the corner near the stove. There is a mouse stuck on the glue trap. Sheeka says, "Oh shit, I finally caught that motherfucker." Sheeka bends down to pick up the trap." This little motherfucker was leaving shit all on my counter and my stove. Little fat bastard ate my lasagna, now I got his ass. Let me throw his ass out." Sheeka walks out of the apartment with the mice in mouse trap. She walks to the garbage dump (incinerator) and throws the mice in. " You want to be in the garbage so much, now your little fat ass can enjoy it." She walks back the apartment. Tawana is walking up the stairs and her and Sheeka make eye-to-eye contact. Tawana says, "Long time no see." Sheeka replies, "What do you want? And how the fuck you know where I live." "You know we know the same people. I just want to talk to you, come here." Tawana reaches for her gun. Sheeka runs into her apartment. Her apartment is right by the stairs. Tawana runs right behind her. Sheeka is trying to close the door but Tawana manages to get half of her body in the door. Tawana forces the door open and she points the gun at Skeeka. Tawana slams the door. Sheeka is backing up down the hallway into the living room. Tawana is walking up the hallway with the gun pointed at Sheeka. They both come into the living room. There are two rug cutter razor blades on the table and Sheeka picks up one backing up. Sheeka says, " I'm not going out like a punk bitch or like the people you done murdered. Tawana points her gun at Sheeka. "Sheeka, Sheeka. You dumb motherfucker. Is your whole family dumb, because your cousin is gonna get her ass killed. You should've told her about being a follower instead of a leader." Tawana pulls the hammer back on the gun. Sheeka says, "You're the one to talk, you followed Amura. So who taught you?" "Fuck you, we make money together and don't forget that is my cousin." "Why don't you put that gun down? You know you can't beat me. I was the Lieutenant. Put it down, lets see whose the baddest bitch. There is another razor right there on the table." Tawana looks at the table. She picks the razor off of the table. She presses a button on the side of her gun and the clip falls out of the gun. She then pulls back the

119

top of the gun and the bullet in the chamber pops out of the gun and falls on the floor. Tawana says, "You know I'm good with this, even though I haven't used one in a long time. I think I was in high school, you was in the principle's office with me." For a quick second they reminisces about when they were in high school. Tawana and Sheeka are sitting in the principle's office. The principle walks in his office. He walks over and stands right in front of Tawana and Sheeka. The Principle says, "Tawana why are you always into fights. You too Sheeka!" Tawana is licking her lips. Tawana says to the principle, "You don't complain when I'm sucking your wife's pussy." "Cut the bullshit, you know damn well you didn't suck my wife's pussy. The security guard said he seen you with a rug cutter." Tawana responds, "I do carpentry." Tawana gets out of the seat and goes in her back pocket and pulls out a rug cutter and slashes the principle across the face. The principle is bleeding screaming for security. The Principle yells, "Some body help me please. The security runs into the office and grabs Tawana. The both come out of that day dream, Tawana and Sheeka stand looking at one another eye to eye. Tawana says, "Do you want to see me cut something?" "Let's see you try." Tawana runs toward Sheeka swinging the rug cutter wildly. Sheeka ducks and cuts Tawana in the face. Tawana touches her face and begins to scream. Tawana shouts, " You fucking bitch, you cut my face. Don't let me grab your ass, once I do that, I'm going to fuck you up. Tawana drops the razor blade on the floor. She gives Sheeka an evil look. She charges at Sheeka and tries to grab her. Sheeka is slicing Tawana in the face with the razor blade. She is bleeding badly. The blood drips from her face. Tawana grabs Sheeka's hand with the razor blade. The razor cuts Tawana's hand. She punches Sheeka in the mouth (repeatedly in different ways). Sheeka spits her blood in Tawana's face. Tawana bends Sheeka's arm and breaks it. Sheeka drops the rug cutter on the floor. Sheeka screams. She punches Sheeka in the face. Sheeka falls on the floor. Tawana spits on her. "You fucking bitch." Tawana turns Sheeka over and sits on her. With her knees on Sheeka's arms. Tawana face is dripping blood from the open wounds on her face. Tawana says, "Now, tell me how that feels. You know, it was pretty fucked up how you went to jail for Amura. "Fuck it. Just do what the fuck you got to do." "I see that smart-ass mouth runs in the family." Tawana reaches for her back up gun. She roles up her left pants. She grabs a Dillinger .45 from the holster strapped on her left leg (shin). She cocks the hammer back. She points the gun at Sheeka. Tawana says, "Do you have anything to say? What's going to be your last words?" Sheeka laughs with her busted lip. Blood is all over her mouth. You remember when we were in high school and I came over to your house for dinner. I was in the bathroom with your father. He was fucking me in my ass and your mother knew about it." Tawana says, "Oh really." Tawana shoots Sheeka in the face." Blood pours from out the back of her head.

★★★

10:00 o'clock that night at Marquis house.

Amura is watching Precious Jewell through the window as she crosses the street to enter Marquis' building. Marquis' body lay dead on the couch. Marquis eyes are open and his mouth is wide open. Beams from the streetlight shines on his body through the blinds hung on the window. Marquis' door opens slowly. The door is open just a little. Precious Jewell walks inside the building where Marquis lives. She walks to the staircase and she looks up. She pulls out her .380 Berretta from her coat pocket. She ejects the clip to see how many bullets are in the clip. Precious Jewell whispers, "Damn, I only got five bullets left." She injects the clip back into the gun. She then pulls the top of the gun back to see if there is a bullet in the chamber. There is a bullet in the chamber. She puts the gun back in her coat pocket. "Good. Those bitches didn't know that I'm the wrong bitch to fuck with." She looks up as she walks up the stairs. She takes a deep breath. She walks up the stairs to the 5th floor. Precious Jewell leans against the wall and she begins to cry. "Maybe I should have listen to Sheeka. I shouldn't have fucked around with Amura." Precious Jewell walks toward Marquis' apartment very slowly. She notices that the door is open and pulls out the gun from her coat pocket. She opens the door. Precious Jewell steps inside the apartment. There is little light. She closes the door and walks down the hallway into the living room. She notices Marquis sitting on the couch. The lights are off. The lights from the outside shines in the room. Amura is looking at Precious Jewell through the cracked door. Amura puts on her leather gloves. The sound of leather being tightly pulled over her hand is heard. Precious Jewell is slowly walking toward Marquis talking to him. "You must have shot up before I got here. Shit, Amura's little bitches are trying to kill me. Have you seen your sister? I want to know if she knows what the fuck is going on. I'm leaving the country. I got a sweet deal with the Africans. On top of the deal we was working out. You should come with me, you don't have to worry about no body telling you that it's bad to shoot-up. We'll stop in Amsterdam; you know they got bars there for us to shoot-up in. Amura is watching Precious Jewell she slowly takes off her shoes. Amura opens the door slowly. She whispers softly. "You fucking bitch. You just don't know that

Marquis was setting your ass up. You don't know what you got yourself into by running your mouth. Precious Jewell walks closer to the body. "Do you hear me talking to you Marquis? Marquis, Marquis." Precious Jewell walks to the couch. Marquis' dead body is facing the other way. Precious Jewell does not know that he is dead. She walks closer to the dead body. She sees that Marquis is dead. She shouts, "No, no, not you." Precious Jewell does not believe what she is seeing. "How could they have done this to you" Amura runs out of the room toward Precious Jewell from behind. "What's up Mrs. Benedict Arnold?" Precious Jewell turns around and she is in shock. Amura punches her in the face. The gun falls out of her hand. Amura punches her in the face again and again and again. Amura knocks her down. Amura walks over to the gun and she picks it up. She pulls the top of the .380 Berretta and all of the bullets eject out of the top of the gun. Precious Jewell face is fucked-up. Her face is swollen and she has blood clots in her eyes. Precious Jewell is very dizzy from the punches to her face. Precious Jewell vision is blurry. Precious Jewell is looking at Amura walking toward her with the gun. Precious Jewell wipes the blood from her mouth. Precious Jewell says, "Fuck you. You motherfuckin right, I made a deal with the Africans me and your brother was going to run our own drug pipeline.

AN EMOTIONAL HOMICIDE

And I told the cops about the whole set up bitch. You let my cousin Sheeka go down for your shit, so it's your time to go down." Amura stands over her with the gun and says, ".Oh really." Amura slaps her in the face with the gun and knocks Precious Jewell out. Precious Jewell has little conscious. "You know what I think, you need another slap across the face." Amura grabs Precious Jewell hair and lifts her head and slaps her on the side of the head. Precious Jewell is completely knocked the fuck out. Everything goes black. Amura drags Precious Jewell on to the couch where Marquis is laying dead from the gunshot wound to the head. Amura sits Precious Jewell right next to Marquis. Amura goes in the room and comes back out with a small zip lock bag of herion. She throws a small zip lock bag of heroin on the table. A syringe, a cigarette lighter a tablespoon, and a bottle of liquor is also on the table. Amura kneels down to the table and picks up the tablespoon and bends it back so it can stand up by itself. Amura twist the top of the liquor bottle and pours the liquor on to the tablespoon. She then opens the zip lock bag and takes a pitch of heroin out and dumps it on the spoon. She reaches for the cigarette lighter. She flicks the lighter to light and puts the flame under the tablespoon until the liquor and heroin comes to a boil. She puts down the lighter. She reaches for the syringe and puts the needle on to the spoon. She injects the heroin into the syringe. Amura says, "Yeah you are going to get high all right. And you will get to meet Bigtime. He wants to see you. It's such a shame the bad guys will walk away once again. They do say bad guys where black and black is my favorite color. Amura puts the syringe on the table. She reaches for Precious Jewell feet. Amura slides both of Precious Jewell shoes off. Precious Jewell is barefooted. Amura begins to suck her toes. She licks to when saliva is seen. Amura reaches for the syringe on the table. Precious Jewell is regaining consciousness. Her eye site is very blurry. Her face is swollen with blood from the punches and the pistol wiping. She stares at Amura. Amura ejects a little bit of the heroin out of the needle. Precious Jewell says, "What are you doing?" Amura replies, " What the fuck it look like I'm doing? You know I don't stick needle in my arm or my neck. This is for you. Some one is coming to see you, so I want you to get a little rest. So take this. Amura jumps toward Precious Jewell and grabs her head back and sticks her in the neck with the syringe. Amura presses down on the syringe injected Precious Jewell with the heroin. Precious Jewell loses consciousness.

★★★

2 hour later
Amura is leaning against the wall with lighter fluid in her hand. Precious Jewell regains consciousness again.

Amura says, "So your ass is finally up. You were knocked out for almost 2 hours." A knock from the door. Knock, knock, knock. Amura is smiling looking at Precious Jewell in a deceitful way. "It's about time he got here." Amura shouts "The door is open." The shoes of a man walking through the door and he closes the door. The man walks down apartment hallway. He is coughing. The man shouts at Amura with a sore throat. "You got anything in here for me to drink." The man coughs. "Damn I need something for this cough." She shouts, "Go in the kitchen, it is some 180 proof vodka on the table in there. That should clear it up. Also, I got your ring out of the sink. It is on the table next to the vodka." He walks into the kitchen and sees the ring and the vodka sitting on the table. He reaches for the ring with his leather gloves on. He takes off his gloves and puts it on his middle finger. He picks up the bottle of liquor and walks out of the kitchen. The man is walking down the hallway into the living room. " Thanks for finding my ring. Shit, a lot of African's died in the mines just to get the diamonds in this ring and on my wrist." He pulls up his sleeve and the diamonds sparkle around his wrist. Amura is standing by the door looking at Precious Jewell. The man walks in the entrance of the living room drinking the liquor from the bottle. His face cannot be seen, only the shape of his face. He speaks. "Is that my baby girl? Come to me Precious." Precious Jewell opens her eyes and her vision is blurry until it comes to. She sees Amura and the man standing together. Amura is in the light but the man's face cannot be seen. "Precious, Precious, get up my dear." Precious Jewell says, "Omar is it you. She begins to cry. "Baby boy is that you. Baby." "Yes baby girl it is I." The man steps in the living room. Right before he steps into the light. Flash backs of the man's life. The first flash back is Amura, Marquis, and O standing in their mother's room when they were kids. Amura in full light, Marquis in half the light, O in the darkness. Second flash is Amura, Marquis and, Bigtime sitting in the car. Bigtime's face was not seen. But it is now. The third flash is Dt. Steele (Bigtime) is on the phone telling Amura that he wants Precious Jewell dead. We see who is the leader of the crew is. O, Dt. Steele, and Bigtime are one person. Precious Jewell sees that it is him. Bigtime says, "Come to me." Bigtime walks toward Precious Jewell and Precious Jewell gets off of the couch and runs to Bigtime. Bigtime and Precious Jewell hugs and kisses one another passionately. Bigtime reaches into his back pocket. Precious Jewell says, "I would never betray thy, I love you baby." Bigtime has a knife in his hand. "I know you wouldn't." He slices Precious Jewell in the throat. Precious Jewell grabs her throat. Blood flows through her fingers. She tries to scream but she can't.

LORENZO ANDREWS

Tears from her eyes fall like a water faucet. Precious Jewell falls back through the glass table. Bigtime turns to Amura. "I'll be back here in the morning to fuck up the investigation. Let's get the fuck out of here." He points to Precious Jewell. "Send this bitch to hell!" Amura says, "Marquis always wanted to be cremated anyway." Amura walks over to her brother and kisses him on the cheek. "I'll miss you." As Precious Jewell speaks her last words. Amura quirks lighter fluid all over Precious Jewell and Marquis' bodies. She reaches for her lighter out of her pocket. She lights her brother on fire and the fire spreads to Precious Jewell. Precious Jewell whispers her last words. It is a mustard seed of life left in Precious Jewell. Amura and Bigtime stands in front of her. Precious Jewell looks at the both of them. Precious whispers, "Mislead, betrayed, and backstabbed. I could have never known, even if it was shown. Being romanced by a woman, being loved by a man. How could I have been so insane? It's such a shame. My heartbeats slow, I know it is time to go. Our lives never coincide, so I die of An *Emotional Homicide*. *Her eyelids close.*

★★★

Some Days Later

Amura, Bigtime, Tasha, Tawana, and Dufour are all in the living laughing talking and drinking wine. Amura is looking in the direction of the TV. She picks up the remote control and turns to world news. The news shows people in Africa. The News Anchor says, "In world news. The HIV epidemic. The HIV plaque has destroyed the human race. Not like it has done to Africa. It has destroyed the essence of the people for decades. Generation of people are gone, and now this. The medication that was sent to help them are destroying them. Wonga. This is a mixture of cocaine and HIV medication". The TV shows African women and men smoking the very HIV medication they sent to help Africans go up in smoke.

AN EMOTIONAL HOMICIDE

Black Raspberry Coming Soon

131

BIOGRAPHY

OF

LORENZO ANDREWS

The author of this book Lorenzo Andrews is from Brownsville, New York. He has lived there most of his life. He is the son of a mother whom he got his ideal of writing An Emotional Homicide. Lorenzo Andrews is a child who survived the 1980s explosion of cocaine into the Black American communities, especially the crack cocaine HIV era to which nearly went off like a nuclear bomb in killing Black Americans. This is where the inspiration comes from in writing this book. To which was written as a screenplay first. One cannot imagine the horror of the Black Americans were walking the streets high on cocaine and dying of a sickness that destroyed one's immune system looking like something out of the walking dead. This sickness was mainly in black African counties, and Black American communities.

Thank you all for reading this book which parallels my life in America.

ORDER FORM

Perfect Pair Publications

Post Office Box 27041

Knoxville, TN 37927

Name: _____ **Doc#**_____

Address: _____

City/State: _____

Zip: _____

QTY	TITLES	PRICES

Shipping & Handling (via U.S. Media Mail): $7.00

TOTAL $_____

FORMS OF ACCEPTED PAYMENTS:

Institutional Checks & Money Orders, all mail in orders take 5-7 Business days to be delivered

★★★

Black Raspberry Coming Soon

THE END

PERFECT PAIR
PUBLICATIONS

www.ingramcontent.com/pod-product-compliance
Lightning Source LLC
Chambersburg PA
CBHW061328050726
47504CB00013B/1555